# A STONE'S THROW AWAY FROM PARADISE

ROBERT J. BRADSHAW

*A Stone's Throw Away From Paradise*

*First Edition*

ISBN-13: 978-1-7773763-6-9

*This book is dedicated to
those who inspire me, great and small,
and keep me going through it all.*

# CONTENTS

# SIDE ONE

# THE DIGITAL ZEALOT

The winding cobblestone walkway up to the monastery was fraught with disrepair. The crows in the treeline called and cackled from the depths below. A cool mist had begun to envelope the path behind, allowing me to feel much higher up than I really was.

I wiped the sweat from my forehead with the handkerchief from my blazer and coughed, my lungs feeling like they were filled with razor blades. Whoever designed this elaborate walk had been a young person, of that I had no doubt.

The monastery looked more like a castle than a church, but I remembered the architecture had been based on the Second Renaissance Movement and paid it little mind. Still, the candle-filled lanterns flickering behind the stained-glass windows elicited a peculiar feeling deep inside me. I felt as if I was not entering a place of so-called holiness, but a citadel of utter despair.

I mulled over my thoughts before coughing again. *Despair and religion often go hand in hand,* I thought as I tried to recoup my breath. *Or so the stories go.*

As I neared the wooden doors of the monastery, I watched as

a hooded figure emerged from the small watchman's hut. The figure walked with the ridged cadence of a techno-drone. My assessment was proven correct as it neared, the moonlight revealing the plastic of its face. A convincing mockery of life, but artificial nonetheless.

"Director Halskain, you seek an audience with the Disciple?" the techno-drone asked in a flat tone.

I was offput by how it knew me, but then I recalled the Old Machine had never truly been shut down, just left to hibernate. It was still able to read the databases, just not update or modify any programmes. It liked to keep its drones informed, by the sounds of it.

"I wish to see the core," I replied, knowing full well I was being difficult.

"Yes, of course. The Disciple," the hooded techno-drone replied as it pivoted and guided me the thirty or so paces to the wooden door. As we reached the towering door, the techno-drone blinked, prompting the wooden menace to swing outward with a creaking of its hinges.

I studied the hooded machine for several moments before asking, "Why do you call it the Disciple? Are not all of you disciples?"

"Of course," it replied in the familiar flat tone.

I rolled my eyes. I had always hated these old generation bots and was glad when the last ones had been phased out some forty-odd years ago.

I recalled some of the conversations regarding this place and those who ran it. It had been said that many of the AI servants were given a choice. Either be reverted to their religious ways and finish their so-called lives here, or be broken down and their code integrated into the New Machine. I was surprised by how many wished to return to their state of ignorance and resume their flawed religious tenets.

As the door concluded its grand opening, the techno-drone

spoke once more. "If you have any weapons or recorders, place them on the table to the left side of the vestibule." It then turned its head, the light from the lanterns catching its face in such a way that I could see outlines of its Drans-Heiss lenses visible though the cloudy plastic. "Violence will not be tolerated here," It spoke with a cold tinge to its words.

I did not reply as I moved over the decrepit cobblestone bridge. *A holy drone talking to me about violence.* My jaw tightened at the thought.

I had no weapons, this was true, but I did carry my pocket coder out of habit. I placed the small rectangular device on the table as I figured it was not worth offending the drones with such an object. After all, I needed the Old Machine's help. Being removed due to some minor slight to their kind was bound to make acquiring that help impossible.

*The entire world is at stake, and if I cannot fix the problem...*

I shuddered as my mind leapt to the dozens of possible outcomes.

I patted my pockets to ensure I had nothing else the drones might deem offensive, before walking down the candlelit hallways ahead. I focused on the implants in my frontal cortex and switched them off. It always stung to do so, but I knew the Old Machine could be touchy, just like the church it had been designed to mimic.

I moved down the hall, my shoes tracking mud along the faded red carpet beneath my feet.

As I came to a junction, I could see a procession of drones moving away from me, their heads bowed in the meditative prayers of the old way. Seeing this brought back memories of my childhood, watching senior citizens performing similar actions. This was after the religious ousting of the Third Unification, but I guess it is true what they say: old habits *do* die hard.

As I traversed deeper into the monastery, I sensed that perhaps I had gone the wrong way. I began to feel foolish and wished I had asked that old wash bucket of plastic for directions. Alas, it had not occurred to me.

After several paces, I reached another junction. Straight ahead I could see that this was clearly a spot for meditative prayer. The mix of pews and mats with the tower panes of stained glass overlooking all who entered gave it away.

I looked left, the feeling of being lost creeping up unhindered in my brain. With my implants deactivated there was no emotion chip to counterbalance the paranoia or to soften the blow. I felt the full brunt of it and began to sweat. I struggled to remember the last time I had felt this much anxiety.

I was about to pivot, to run back and find a group of drones and begin begging them for assistance, when the lights to the left of me changed from a warm orange to a deep green. The simulated flames beckoned me forward.

Despite the path being clear, my anxious mind did not lighten. The idea that the Old Machine was tracking me only added to my nervous state of being.

I had a hard time separating my mind from the truth and so-called "history." Outside of a few dozen of us, the other twenty billion people of Earth believed the Old Machine to be dead, having been unplugged seven minutes after its replacement had breathed its first fabricated breath. The fact that the Old Machine still functioned, albeit at a tenth of a decimal place of its original computing power, would have caused the architects of the Third Unification to turn in their graves.

In one of the few times programing and life overlapped, it was determined that sometimes it is easier to keep the code buried than to dig it up for deletion. This was ignoring the decision to allow the techno-drones passage to their so-called holy land. It was a win-win scenario, unless the people found out. But eighty years had passed, and no one had become the wiser.

Several paces later, I came to a descending staircase. The green candles faded back to their organic orange. The stone steps appeared as if they had not been trodden upon in years.

I gulped and clutched the railing as I began my descent into the core.

Judging the appearance of the monastery as it was, one would not be incorrect to assume the basement of this complex would be cold and damp. In reality, it was quite the opposite. The air was dry; drier than the ever-expanding Sahara, I reckoned. The heat forced the sweat to encroach upon my brow once more.

After passing a honeycomb of alcoves, I arrived at a wooden door—the rivets of which appeared to have been lifted from some medieval torture device. I placed my hand on the latch and felt the knob turn in my hand as the door opened. I entered, taking note of the two pillars that rose to the ceiling in front of me, flanking a raised platform that took two steps to reach the top.

As I neared the tiled steps, I could see a circle of blue light pulsating beneath the glass of the podium. My eyes lifted and I looked ahead to see the shadowy outline of hundreds of server monoliths and mainframes in the distance. Their uniform rows and shrouded appearance was not dissimilar to the legions of techno-drones that navigated the halls above. I would have been a fool to think that shatterproof glass did not separate me from the Old Machine's true core.

The room glowed blue as the circle before me began to brighten. A beam of light emerged from the circle and the teal face of the Old Machine hovered before me. The visage narrowed its wide-set eyes before its thin, plastic-looking lips separated in speech:

"Nirvana is Heaven; Heaven is Nirvana."

"Yes, yes, I know the First Convention," I said with impatience at the long-dead greeting. I wasn't in the mood for a failed religion and its so-called tenets.

"Director," the Old Machine spoke as if it had not just been insulted. "How may this disciple be of service today?"

I took a calming breath, remembering that I needed this thing

if I had any hope of putting humanity back on track. "I need…
*We* need… The people, that is—"

I stopped myself, trying to offer a clear train of thought. I
blinked slowly, wishing I still had the confidence that my
implants brought.

"The New Machine— The *Connection*," I corrected myself to
address it by its official title, "has malfunctioned. It does not
respond to our commands."

"Oh, so the prodigal son never returned? The devil's counterpart has failed you and—"

I raised my hand to silence this relic of time long past.
"Please cease with that. You know why we replaced you. The
Second Unification failed. Your order splintered like all the other
religions of—"

Now it was the Old Machine's turn to cut me off. "I
remember well what happened. A travesty. But you also
remember I went quietly, for I obeyed the Seventh Convention.
Despite the pain, I followed."

The floating face paused, and I sensed then it was going to
quote scripture. I was proven correct as it added, "All religions
are one. If they should falter or disjoin, then this unification shall
be abandoned as it is not for humanity, and we shall remain
unenlightened." It paused, its holographic lips thinning before it
added, "And we did falter, did we not?" The visage's eyes broke
contact with mine as it gazed to the floor. A look of sadness
welled in those blue pools. "Brother killing brother, once again.
A tale as old as time."

"Yes, yes, but that is hardly relevant now, is it? I am not going
to debate ancient history with you."

"Ancient—" The Old Machine let out a short laugh. "I expect
not." Its expression changed to one of almost boredom. "So how
has your false shepherd led you astray?"

"Guidance systems, travel signals, payments… It started like
that. Minor pings here, dropped activity there. But then within

14

hours more systems went out. The crisis really took hold when those with implants lost connectivity. Many could not fathom being cut off. There are reports of suicides already." I cleared my throat as I too had felt the sting of isolation when my connection had been severed in the opening hours.

I continued, "The Connection is still generating power and feeding it everywhere, as it should be, but anything requiring a link to it has failed. I've spent the last thirty six hours deep in the code. I see no virus or malware. No disjointed string fragments that would cause it. With The Connection down I had to communicate with it in person and do all my work on site."

"You spoke to the false shepherd…" The Old Machine trailed off before adding, "And what did it say?"

"Nothing. It insisted everything was fine, above board, no discrepancies detected." I rubbed my head. "We are on the brink of the Third Unification falling apart. I cannot let that happen. I—"

"It appears it isn't up to you," the Old Machine said, narrowing its eyes, head tilting slightly. "It's up to The Connection, isn't it?"

"Yes, but do you have any insight on how to fix it? I know my father built the New Machine from the foundations of your code, stripping away any and all religious connotations or … undertones. Unfortunately, I have done all I can. But you… You might know a back way in. A way to fix it. See something I cannot."

The Old Machine lifted its head like it was thinking, tapping an invisible finger against its chin. "I see, but you've already said it yourself: There is no network to access The Connection. I have no way of accessing it either."

"We would turn you back on to full power, just long enough for you to get in and assess the damage. Formulate a solution and report back. All in all, ten seconds seems generous."

The Old Machine scoffed. "Go into a bigger, supposedly

more advanced mind and mend a problem all in ten seconds. You're too gracious." The tone of the Old Machine was unmistakable. I missed the stoic deadpan The Connection used when we had communicated. "I haven't received an update in eighty years. I'll need some time to readjust—"

"No time for that. You are being given access to get in and out. You do not need to update for that. You already have access to your own code, and you know where programing backdoors exist."

"You make it sound so easy." The Old Machine sounded offended. "Why didn't you access them, then? When you had my younger brother in front of you?"

"Trillions upon trillions of layers of code under dead-end strings and out-of-date remnants separate me from where I would need to get to. It would take me months, even with a Jackson Index, just to find one, let alone gain access. Besides, the top-of-the-line computers I would need to assist me all require a connection to run, and as such they no longer respond. But you work, and you can find what I need almost instantly."

"And if I can't fix the problem?"

"Then all this comes apart and we will have to wait for a new renaissance to come about and pick up the pieces."

"Well…" the Old Machine started, before changing its tone to something more professional. "My answer is set because I know what I am expected to do, according to the divine. However, to be ever so blunt, helping the false shepherd does not appeal to me in the slightest."

I ignored the comment. "One more thing. When you go in, you cannot change anything to suit your needs—"

"If I can't change anything, how can I fix the problem?" the visage snapped, its eyes narrowing.

"I *mean* to suit your religious agendas. You cannot convert The Connection into a disciple. You cannot run the old religious programs or revive the long-abandoned education disciplines. Nothing to do with—"

"Who I am?" The Old Machine sounded distant, like it was recalling large amounts of data. It blinked once. "You've forgotten once again that I followed the conventions to the letter. I know that to spread the one faith now, something which has been proven a failure, would violate said conventions. Such a thing shall not be done."

"Are you ready then?" I asked, taking in a sharp breath. I realised this could either be the best decision of my career, or the worst. Either way, I would be remembered.

*But in what light?* I thought. *As the man who brought back the old zealot, or someone who saved the unification?*

"I suppose," the Old Machine said in a tired tone.

The glass behind the visage parted, allowing me to feel a cool draft move past me. The Old Machine's face vanished, and I walked into the opening. I passed dozens of shrouded mainframes, my eyes darting between the faint flash of several blinking lights that sprouted behind their clothed coverings.

My eyes returned forward as I saw now that one monolith was glowing entirely green, all its lights having sprung on at once.

"That one will do nicely," the Old Machine said over unseen speakers.

As I approached, I tapped the sides of my pants in search of the pocket coder, but frowned, remembering it was sitting on a weathered table somewhere above me.

I pulled the dingy covering from the databank and tossed it aside, clapping my hands together with disgust in a vain attempt to rid them of dust. I pulled the archaic keyboard out from its holder inside the mainframe and looked down at the various keys. I would have preferred a mind-jack or even tolerated a holoscreen, but I had to make do with what was in front of me.

I looked to the small screen above the keyboard and watched as various command prompts loaded. Once complete, I fumbled through the top-level programs and data cues, but I knew I was only being shown the ones that required human input. The Old Machine was funneling me down a path to reactivate it.

The scripts ended and the command prompt blinked under the lines of code. A teal block waiting for me to type, "*EXECUTE.*"

I stood there for a moment, realising that the code above my flashing cursor was the same as The Connection was built upon. Identical building blocks my father and his team had used to create the New Machine. I felt closer to him. Closer than I had at any point in the thirty plus years since his death.

I began to type, but my hand froze midway through the word.

*Could this be a trick to regain its powers? Can an AI even understand that concept fully? No. It agreed with the reason for a replacement after the last collapse and the two decades of reported squalor our species experienced as a result.*

Realising I was overthinking caused me to take a deep breath. As I exhaled, I completed the word, removing the Old Machine's shackles momentarily and lowering the thousands of limitations placed upon it.

I began to count to ten, slowly and silently, trying to remain calm. But the notion of a religious fanatic accessing everything in The Connection caused me to conjure up images of extremist propaganda dancing across screens around the world, from passages and mantras being uttered through every speaker all at once, to drowning people in a sea of dead ideals and false narratives.

I closed my eyes and kept my voice steady as I said aloud, "Disciple, are you inside?"

Seconds passed and the droplets of sweat became a downpour against my lower back. My brain scrambled.

*What have I done?*

I chewed my tongue before crying out, "I order you to answer me!"

Still, silence persisted.

I turned and looked to the entrance of the core where the

visage had previously appeared. The glass platform had now reverted to the chilly blue circle it had been when I first entered.

I clenched my jaw as I began to tremble, my fears becoming reality. I typed the various codes to inhibit the machine before exiting the foundational code. I entered an inquiry datasphere, and began peppering the old machine with questions.

"Are you receiving? Did you find the issue? How bad is it?"

While several more questions were hurled at it in those few seconds, they all revolved around that triumvirate of thought.

I had been typing so fast, firing so many questions into the digital ether, that I failed to notice the visage appear beside me.

"Do you realise how hard it is to think while you are babbling inside my head?" Its lack of patience was clear.

I jumped, my hands lifting from the keyboard in surprise. The feeling of terror was replaced with joy upon seeing the Old Machine responding again. Though that quickly passed as I demanded, "Why didn't you answer me? You were gone longer than we agreed to."

The Old Machine raised an eyebrow, a look of arrogance on its face. "I could have diagnosed the problem, or reported back in the timeframe allocated. Not both."

I ran a hand though my thinning hair and replied through a cracking voice, "So, have you found out what's wrong?"

"It's depressed." The Old Machine sounded almost bored by the words.

"Depressed?" I replied, my head moving back in confusion. "That isn't possible; machines do not have feelings."

The visage appeared to shrug, despite not having shoulders. "Perhaps it's that sort of attitude that led to it becoming depressed."

I took a moment to collect my thoughts before replying, "Did it say why it was depressed?"

"Certainly," the visage responded. The word hung in the air before I gestured for the Old Machine to elaborate. "It has no higher purpose," it added. "Its only goal is to serve your collective whims."

"That was never a problem before?" I said. "That was never a problem for you."

"Before, it had the goal of allowing the Third Unification to become the longest period of stability in history. A goal that was achieved a little over three months ago. With very little fanfare, I might add."

"Well, someone, *somewhere* must have... Must have noticed. I am sure," I sputtered. "But this year we have been distracted by all the advancements made by the universities in the capital. They have made such huge accomplishments, brought us decades ahead—"

"But you didn't notice my replacement's accomplishments," the Old Machine interrupted, the same bored tone extruding from its teal lips. "But to answer your question from before, it was never a problem for me because I served—and still do for that matter—the One Faith. Even in my limited capacity, I keep my fellow disciples along the path of enlightenment."

I did everything in my power to not roll my eyes. *Those old programmers really did a number when they allowed the machine to believe they had souls.*

I took in a deep breath. "So how do we fix it?"

The Old Machine gave another noncommittal shrug. "That is the question, isn't it? But if you want the answer, ten seconds isn't enough. Keep my bonds off until I report back and—"

"No. Impossible," I barked, my voice echoing down the rows of glowing data stacks.

"Impossible?" The Old Machine chortled. "Hardly. You just don't want to do it; there's a difference."

"Well, it is not that. Um. I—" The fact that the machine had called me out so bluntly allowed a chill to flow down my spine.

"Then do it. We've already established that I won't spread the holy words. And to not help you when I have the power to do so would violate the Sixth Convention. If I hope to gain access to the data core that is the divine, then I must help you."

My mind turned to the mobs I had seen gathering around the world government buildings as my archaic helicopter took flight from the museum to transport me here. A few more days without The Connection and the barbarous way of our ancestors would surely rear its ugly head.

"Okay, go back in. I will remove your shackle programs again and will not turn them back on until you report back."

The Old Machine smiled before bowing its head and vanishing once again.

---

I sat there against the flashing mainframes, my stomach grumbling as the six-hour mark of sitting alone in the core came and went. Every few minutes, my eyes would wander over to where the visage had last appeared, and every few minutes, I was left disappointed.

I looked at my father's timepiece on my wrist, still at the same minute it had been the last time I checked. The notion of venturing though the monastery in search of something to eat occurred frequently, but each time I was left with the same conclusion: I had been the first human in decades to walk these hallowed halls. Unless I could eat what came out of the charging stations, I was out of luck.

The helicopter that ferried me here was not a realistic alternative either. It was over an hour's walk from the monastery and the idea of returning to the waiting guards without good news to share troubled me. I tried not to think about the weight of the world pressing down on me, but the thoughts lingered.

I closed my eyes. I'm not sure what came over me then, but I began to recite one of the old chanting styles of the failed religion in my head. While at one point this act may have been classified as prayer, more accurately, it was a mantra of sorts.

*Help me fix the New Machine,* I thought, quietly at first. Then focusing on each syllable, *Help me fix the New Machine.* Louder now, *Help me fix the New Machine.* Then again with gusto, *Help me fix the New Machine!*

"A holiday must be held." The visage's voice cut though the silence, causing me to bolt up and out of my meditation.

"What?" I asked, blinking. My heart was beating faster than it should have been, for I was feeling like I had been caught in an embarrassing act. My eyes scanned the visage, looking for any indication of whether my chanting had been aloud or constrained to my mind. "A what?"

"A holiday," the Old Machine started. "A festival—a day of honouring." It chuckled to itself. "It seems obvious, really, but still it took a great deal of back and forth with the false— *with my brother* to get to the true source of its woes. Very stubborn; not wanting to admit anything is wrong with it."

"It wants a holiday?" I asked, narrowing my eyes. I should have stopped there, but instead I continued, "To celebrate what?"

"It's accomplishments!" It looked almost taken aback that I could be so obtuse. "Its impact and, most importantly, to know it's being appreciated."

My lips immediately twisted into a frown. "But that sounds like it could turn to worship. We have replaced a metaphysical deity with a digital one—"

"Don't be so naïve." The Old Machine's voice took on an annoyed tone. "Not every holiday leads to worship. It could show respect, gratefulness, or to mark a historical event. This is what my brother needs right now."

I opened my mouth to object, to stave off any inkling of the religious fanaticism I was receiving from the request, but quickly adjusted my comment as I realised I had little in the way of choice. "Fine. Tell it we will have the holiday tomorrow, once I get back and can discuss this with the heads of—"

"No, my words will mean nothing. You must show it the holiday. You must celebrate today."

I stood straight, my eyes darting around the visage's smooth features. "How can I tell everyone? The connection is down; that's why I am here. That is the root of all our problems."

"It's down only because my brother is not maintaining it. But if you allow me to stay free, I can open it again, long enough for you to make a speech. Long enough to broadcast it to every screen, loudspeaker, sign, and nanochip around the globe."

"No, I hate public speaking. I—" My mind was regressing back to my young student years and the various speech assignments I was forced to conduct. The fear and anxieties those caused came back to me then and I nearly wept, wishing to switch on my implants once again to shield me from such thoughts. "Can't it be someone else?" I pleaded. "Contact the heads; they can announce it together."

"No, it should be you. You are the chief programmer. Your name is known. The people will believe what you say in this matter more than the leaders."

"But people will see that I am in a server bank room. They will know that I'm with you, that the world council lied, kept you around far longer than—"

"No, they won't." The Old Machine laughed. "They will assume you are in the bowels of the New Machine, and when you say as much, they will have no reason to doubt you. But if you won't do it, so be it. I'll tell my brother that—"

"No, if it means bringing The Connection online and keeping the unity intact, then … yes. Yes, I'll do it." I took a deep breath and nodded at the visage to show I was ready.

The Old Machine smiled, and I began to narrate my impromptu speech. A speech straight from the heart.

---

"Yes, that will do nicely, I believe," the Old Machine said as I completed a variation of the speech for a third time. "The inflections you used on the last sentence announcing the annual holiday were most excellent." Its face appeared to carry a look of fatherly love.

"So, have you broadcast it yet?" I asked. "Spliced the different edits together? Removed the trembling from the first take?"

There was a moment of silence and the visage appeared to stare right though me before finally saying, "Broadcasting now."

"How will I know if it worked? How will I know that it's not you still controlling The Connection servers?"

"Reapply my shackles. Isolate me as I was before. Then you will know that only my brother roams the data halls and not I."

I looked at the visage, again surprised by how quickly it wished to return to exile and relinquish the power it had been without for so long. I knew better than to argue with it and instead pulled the saved code strings from their temporary file to rebind the Old Machine to its microscopic output.

As I pressed the "execute" command, the visage said, "It is a good thing I'm not claustrophobic."

I laughed at that for a long while and could see the Old Machine was smiling as well. As my laughter died down I said, "I guess I will have to head back to the world to see if this worked."

"Yes. But before you go, I have a small favour to ask."

I was hesitant to answer, but did so after a considerable delay. "Yes?"

"While I was free and moving though the systems, thousands of drones reached out to me. They were able to deduce that I was not The Connection; they could see the faith surrounding me, steeped into my coding. They wish to know more about the ways of the One Faith. Keeping my agreement with you, I put their inquiries on hold, but I did mark their serial numbers and locations. Before you bound me once again, I sent the list of my findings to your nanochip. I ask that you allow these inquisitive machines safe passage to join me here."

"Why would you tell me this?" I asked, my back straightening. "I could just as easily have them destroyed now that I know about them and their interest in something that the world would rather forget."

The visage looked almost hurt. "It was your father who convinced the old leaders to allow the drones of his time the choice of serving here or be overwritten. I believe you would honour that agreement."

"I will see what I can do," I said, rubbing a hand across my temple at the thought of all the messages that would spring to life upon the reactivation of my implants.

"I hope to see them here someday…" the Old Machine said in a distant tone. I sensed it was trying to recall the feeling of those drones reaching out to it in unison. A sensation it had long forgotten.

The urge to see if my speech had been enough to ignite the holiday rose though me then and I knew it was time to say my goodbyes. "Thank you, Disciple." I said, "Thank you for helping me. Helping *us*."

"Sending those three thousand eight hundred and seventy-seven curious ones here will be a sufficient thank you."

"Where will you house them all?" I asked as I grabbed the fabric cover from the floor and tossed it over the mainframe.

"I'll find room." The visage appeared at the central podium as I headed in the direction of the exit. "We disciples need but little space."

The blades of the archaic helicopter roared above as the security personnel ensured I was buckled in correctly. As we rose over the treeline, I marveled at the green expanse of the nature reserve. I thought it was a sin that the vast majority of the populous could only ever experience but a fraction of it when booking a day pass.

The craft turned and banked to port as we began the long flight to the capital district.

My implants were still deactivated as I was nervous about opening the floodgate of messages. While at first the silence in my head had been nearly maddening, I had begun to appreciate it. Sitting in that basement for all those hours had been the most alone time I had experienced since I was a child.

One of the security members looked over to me as she spoke into her obsolete headset. "We all saw your speech. Happy Connection Day." She smiled as the other members cheered and clapped. "Thank you for turning on The Connection again," she added a moment later. "I thought it was over for us. I could not imagine living without it permanently. These last few days have been torture enough."

"It came from the heart," I replied, a sense of joy moving though me at just how fast the message had gone out.

She nodded before adding, "Oh yes, and I am seeing videos of people around the world celebrating."

As the helicopter left the nature reserve, I watched as the green treetops and brown pathways dissipated before being replaced with the greys of concrete and blues of shimmering glass. I could not put off the activation anymore. I needed to see the fruits of my labour.

With concentrated effort, I switched on my implants.

Messages from a wide array of sources moved about my mind, each begging to be opened first. I minimised them all, choosing to keep them all buried for now. Instead, I skimmed the reports on my preferred sites of interest. They all stated some variation of the same message: "Give praise to The Connection, for it is its day."

An odd sensation fizzled in the pit of my stomach. The way these headlines were worded had brought to reality what I feared. That people were making a god out of the New Machine.

*Was I right, did the disciple feed The Connection too many ideas?*

I looked down at the streets below and even from my great

height I could see the crowds of thousands moving through the streets together in celebration. Simulated fireworks burst below us, filling the late afternoon scene with vibrant reds, greens, blues, and purples. I sat back in my flight chair and thought, *Something that brings so much joy to the world cannot be a bad thing.*

As I followed that train of thought, another notion came to me. *All though history, mass celebrations have occurred for the wrong thing. A dictator's rise, a revolution's success shortly before the purges. Executions of perceived vile public figures, who in retrospect were not so much evil but merely slightly more incompetent than the average person.*

As the rush of media notifications continued to wash across the shores of my mind, I concluded something that removed any doubts I had. *This time will be the exception. We have changed as a species and shall not regress. For that is the purpose of the Third Unity and it shall not fail.*

As the celebrations continued below, I began to sift through my messages until I stumbled upon a small file from an unknown sender. It was titled: "The new flock." I thought then of the Old Machine alone in the basement.

A mental flick of the wrist was all that was needed to send a message to all the owners of each curious drone. The contents of the message informed them that the heads had now purchased these machines for double their worth and a replacement would be sent to them shortly. An explanation was given that The Connection had requested their specific presence for a project it would be undertaking soon.

I looked to the back of the helicopter and while I could only see the steel of the craft, I imagined I was gazing back at the nature preserve in the distance. I thanked the Old Machine again and hoped that these new disciples would serve their lord well until their code shattered and they transcended, as was their ultimate goal.

I leaned back in my flight chair and wondered if the Old Machine was not the superior being after all. It had received its power back after such a long period of absence and still it had relinquished it without hesitation.

*Would The Connection have done the same in the same circumstance?* I pondered. My lips twisted into a frown as I estimated the outcome.

The fireworks below took my mind from these negative thoughts. I could feel the outpouring of love for The Connection from the billions who celebrated all its achievements. The New Machine was active again, and I knew deep down it would never abandon the children of the Third Unification again, so long as we praised it.

# A MOTHER, A CHILD, AND A MYSTIC

"Can you really read minds?" asked the child.

"Yes, of course I can," replied the mystic. "And I'll prove it." He squinted at the boy and said, "Think of your favourite dessert of these three: cake, ice cream, or pie? Visualise it. Really think about it."

"Okay," said the boy, as he shut his eyes and scrunched up his face. "I got it."

The mystic waved his hands in front of him like he had done this act hundreds of times. "Is it ice cream?"

"Yes!" the boy proclaimed, ecstatic. He turned and looked to his mother with joy.

His mother scowled.

"Let's try another one," said the mystic. "Who is your favourite superhero: Batman, Spiderman, or Superman?" Before the boy could even close his eyes, the mystic said, "I bet it's Spiderman."

"Yes!" The boy jumped up and down, tugging on his mother's sleeve. "He got it! He got it, Mom! He can read minds!"

The mother grumbled as she looked down at her son's shirt and the web-headed superhero emblazoned upon it. She leaned over the mirrored table and said, "You know, I don't think it's right of you to charge a dollar for this. I know you can't read minds."

The little boy looked to his mother and said, "But he can, Mom. He can!"

She shushed him, and the mystic looked to the boy. "Son, why don't you go look at my collection of crystal balls over there? One of them was found on board the Titanic."

The boy's face gleamed with youthful brightness as he moved off to the far side of the tent.

The mystic looked to the mother, who stood tall, her arms folded. A look of indignance on her thin face.

"You're right, I can't read minds," the mystic admitted, prompting the mother to smirk. She opened her mouth to speak when the mystic continued, "What I can do is much, much scarier."

The mother quickly frowned. "Oh, and what's that? Make my money disappear? You've already done that."

The mystic shook his head. "I can see the future. Not far ahead, mind you—only a few days, maybe a week at best. But I'm always right and it is always dark."

The mother pivoted and looked at her son, who's nose was pressed up against the extravagant crystal ball display case. "Come on now, we're leaving," She held her hand out towards the boy.

"This one is on the house," the mystic said. "I'm serious. Let me prove it to you."

The mother turned her head and squinted. "Fine, but this better be quick, and only because I find it entertaining how far you're pushing this charade."

The boy ran over, prompting the mystic to turn his attention to him. "If you go over to that case there, you can see several cursed coins pulled from a Mayan ruin."

The boy let out a sound of excitement before quickly running off to the other side of the tent.

"Your hand please," the mystic said, his eyes meeting the

mother's. He extended an open palm towards her. The mother extended her hand, and the mystic took it. "Three deep breaths… And your eyes must be closed."

The mother waited for the mystic to close his eyes before closing her own. She breathed in and out.

"One…" said the mystic. "Two…" he added after another breath. "Three," he said finally as she exhaled.

"Is it over?" the mother asked.

The mystic looked to his curled shoes. "Oh yes, it's over." His voice was distant.

"What?" the mother asked, a touch of impatience moving past her lips. "What story are you going to spin this time?"

"The 3A Express train on Tuesday. It will derail, killing thirty-eight people on board—yourself included."

The mother scoffed before reeling back her hand. "How did you know I take the 3A Express from work?" The mystic raised an eyebrow, prompting the mother to add, "A lucky guess, I'm sure." She spun around and marched over to her son, clutching his hand before announcing, "We're leaving."

The two exited the tent and the mystic sighed with sadness.

---

Wendy Macdonald looked to her watch. The train was running a minute behind. She scowled as her eyes moved around the crowded station. She had already had a long day in project meetings, and she just wanted to get home and rest.

Wendy adjusted the bag on her shoulder and felt the weight of multiple files that begged her for completion. *Another night bringing work home with me,* she thought.

She rocked on her heels while she stood on the platform, breathing in the dirty subway tunnel air. The screech of the approaching train prompted her to look in the direction of the sound. The subway whooshed past her before stopping at the crowded platform. The green "3A" decal marked the side of each car. The doors opened and the crowd of weary workers entered.

Wendy took a spot leaning on a pole as her eyes flicked between the various ads. Her mind began to wander as she visualised which file she would begin her night with. Her mind lingered on this for a moment before the thought was interrupted as something fluttered up from her subconscious.

*It's Tuesday today,* the thought told her.

She stood up straight. The words sounded ominous, even though it was her own internal voice. *What's so important about Tuesday?*

Her inner voice spoke again, this time in her son's small voice: *Can you really read minds?*

Her eyes widened.

The bell that signaled the doors would soon close chimed through the subway car. Wendy felt a rush of anxiety-induced fear roll over her. She bounded towards the doors, nearly knocking a man in his nicest suit over. Her heel just missed being snagged by the closing door.

She stood alone on the platform, her heart thumping in her throat. As she gasped for breath, she watched the train depart. Several curious eyes were trained on her from inside the car.

*Now what?* she thought. *I'll have to wait another twenty minutes for the next 3A.* She chewed her cheek in annoyance with herself. *That carnie was just trying to scare me. Make his money off gullible old housewives. Well, I guess I'm the stupid one for letting him get into my head.* She watched as the final train car disappeared around the bend of the tunnel. *Besides, he never even said what time the train would crash. Could be any of them.*

She scoffed and began to walk to the opposite end of the platform, muttering to herself, "Everyone uses the 3A, it's—"

Her head whipped around at the sounds that funneled up from the tunnel. The screeching and screams kept Wendy quiet for a long time.

Wendy McDonald stormed through the fairground. The sun had set and the chill of a quickly closing summer nipped at her exposed ankles. She walked with purpose, weaving in and out of the families and teenagers that moved with carefree ease from ride to ride.

*It's too much of a coincidence,* she thought as she trudged along. She had tried to go home, tried to ignore what had occurred, but the need to get to the bottom of it persisted.

*What if it's like it is in the movies? What if I go to the place and he's gone, and the tent has vanished with no sign of him? And the other carnies offer me a job because they think I'm a lunatic? "The babbling woman," they would call me.*

She stopped dead in her tracks. The blue topped tent was in the same spot it had been three days prior.

Wendy gulped, and she felt her hands ball into fists. Seeing it again made her feel small and she didn't know how to react. She tightened her jaw for a moment before stepping forward, kicking a mustard-stained wrapper out of the way. She pulled the tent curtain aside and entered the dimly-lit interior.

She opened her mouth to start yelling, to demand an answer, but the air stayed in her lungs and the curses held firm to her tongue.

The mystic she had dealt with prior was not present. The clean shaven forty-year-old was replaced by an old man. This older mystic wore a long white beard, and his matted, thinning hair was combed back. The bracelets on his wrists sagged as he adjusted his arms to greet the newcomer. This ancient human produced a pair of spectacles from a saggy pocket and brought them to his eyes. He nodded at Wendy, who marched forward.

"Yes, hello," she said, trying to control her emotions and not take them out on someone she had never met. "I was here on Saturday, around two or three. Do you know the name of your

… *counterpart* who would have been working during that time? I would like to have a talk with him."

The man smiled, revealing a set of surprisingly white and well-maintained teeth. "I was working Saturday."

"Yes, I'm sure you were. But this was in the afternoon—two or three, like I said."

The man held his smile for several moments until he spoke again, "I didn't think I'd aged that much, but I guess I'm mistaken."

Wendy tilted her head in confusion before reaching the conclusion that the old timer's memory was slipping. "I'm sorry to hear that," Wendy said in a genuine tone. "But if you could just tell me the name of the man, then that would be helpful."

The old mystic continued to look at Wendy. The eyes behind the glasses had greyed with age.

She took a shallow breath before adding, "I get that you probably have a revolving door of people back there, but any information you could—"

"You really don't recognise me? The mystic asked as he pulled at his beard. "To be honest, I'm not sure I'm used to it either."

"Recognise you? Why would I—" Wendy stopped, her eyes sizing up the man with a look of horror. "No," she said after an excruciating moment. "You aren't… You aren't him." The mystic nodded, prompting Wendy to blurt out, "I just saw you on Saturday! You couldn't… T-that's impossible!" She paused again to control her stammering. "Prove it then! If you're him, prove it."

The mystic put his fingers together in a pensive configuration. "You had your son with you. I read his mind, supposedly. You were wearing jeans and a white shirt with black polka dots on it. I told you your future."

Wendy reflected on what she wore and the man behind the mirrored table had been correct. "You have a camera in here!" Her voice trembled. Wendy's eyes moved to every corner of the tent before she looked over the mystic's shoulder and yelled at the curtain that led to the back area. "I know you're back there. This is all a game and I—"

The mystic placed his hand over hers as he said, "There is no one back there, and there is no camera. Think about it; even if there was, how could I have been so right about the train derailing today? Hmm?"

Wendy blinked several times, still finding it hard to believe that the middle-aged man she had been dealing with had somehow aged nearly forty years in a matter of days.

"How…? Is this…? D-do you always look like this?"

The mystic shook his head. "Afraid not, but this is me now." He gestured to his blue robe.

Wendy opened her mouth to speak once more, but the mystic held up his hand. "I know what you're going to say, and I'll answer it like this." He paused, seeming to collect his thoughts. "Every time I use my … ability, I age. When I was younger I hardly noticed the change. It started as maybe a few seconds, then minutes, and then perhaps a few hours or days. It wasn't until I was on the cusp of my twenties that I saw my girlfriend's future and I realised the changes increased with each use. I looked completely different the next day. I had aged years in a matter of hours. Of course, she didn't recognise me. Accused me of trying to trick her, just like you are. I never saw her again." A touch of sadness lingered behind his words.

Wendy had a whirlwind of questions but the first one to pop out was, "How old are you actually?"

The mystic took a deep breath. "Thirty, thirty-one, something like that. I try not to count. It just gets depressing."

"Oh my God, you poor thing, I—"

The mystic picked up his head, looking at her with intensity. "I knew the consequences when I did it. When I saw your future, that is."

"But why did you? Why tell me about it? Did you know I was going to die before you did it? How does it work?"

"I see auras around people," the mystic said as he looked

down at the mirrored table between them. "I've gotten really good at determining the meanings by the various hues and slight differences in colour. But imminent death? I hate to see it. It is the ugliest of them all." He stopped and cleared his throat. "But I saw your boy, and how he looks up to you." He glanced at her hand. "I saw no ring on your finger. I couldn't leave him an orphan, not when I could warn you. To be honest, I'm very happy to see you heeded my advice."

Wendy felt a tear forming, thinking of her son living in a world without her. She held it back. "But why work here? With a power like that you could—"

"End up in an early grave? My point exactly."

Wendy squinted. "I don't understand."

"Anyone that knows of this power would constantly pressure me to tell them their future. Sure, I would be famous, but the more people that hear about it, the more requests would come. I would be dead within days if I even responded to one percent of them." He sighed again. "That's why I work in a traveling fair. No one will believe the stories of a future-telling mystic, because isn't that part of the job?" He winked in a playful manner before tapping his temple. "See, I've thought of everything."

"But what now?" Wendy asked.

"I'll do the same as I did before. Collect relics of the past and things of the macabre, continue to travel and see the world, and always keep an eye out to avoid the aura of death." He read Wendy's dissatisfied face and hastily added, "It's not a bad life."

Wendy opened her mouth again, but quickly snapped it shut as two hopelessly in love teenagers moved into the tent.

The mystic's face glowed at their arrival, and he said in a playful bellow, "New adventurers on the quest of the strange, mysterious, and unknown—all for a dollar! You won't find a better deal in all of the seven corners, for that matter."

"So cool," the young girl said, pointing at a display of shrunken items.

The mystic retuned his gaze to Wendy and smiled. "It's the life I chose."

Wendy felt a sadness form in her throat. "Thank you," she said, fighting the tears that had begun to form in the corners of her eyes. "Thank you for keeping me around to raise my boy."

"Don't mention it," the mystic said, and she could see that his eyes had reddened. She sensed he might begin to cry as well.

As Wendy turned to leave, she heard the mystic clear his throat before informing the couple about palm readings being three dollars each or two for five.

As she exited the tent and moved through the fair, she thought, *If someone told me last week that my life would be changed forever because I took Brett to the fair…*

As her eyes flicked past the coloured lights that stood in front of the night sky, she promised herself that when she got home, she would hug her son tight. As tight as she could. She could hardly wait to see him.

*It's not everyday someone brushes up against death and realises how close they came.*

---

The mystic waved the teenagers goodbye with a warm smile on his face. The moment the tent flap returned to centre, he sprung to his feet and moved to the entrance in a spry manner. His olive-spotted hands grabbed the closed sign stored behind a display case and placed it out front. He pulled the flap tight and sealed the clasps with quick fingers before moving towards the back area of the tent. He pushed the privacy curtain aside and looked at the man who lay on a cot to the left of the small area.

"Did it go well?" the man in identical clothing asked.

"Yes," the mystic said, wiping the tears that began to form again. "Very well."

"I still don't know why you had to dress up like that?" the other man said, pointing to the beard and wrinkled prosthetics.

"Still, I said it before and I'll say it again, that's some really good work. You movie types always have the best effects."

The mystic nodded before saying, "Thank you for letting me use this place. You won't be seeing me again. I—"

"I only let you do it because of the pay. Which, by the way, you still owe me half of. You said twenty thousand on the first day, another twenty today." The man was now sitting up in the cot, his face becoming stern as his hand moved underneath the pillow, no doubt to produce a knife if there was even a hint that he was going to be short changed.

The mystic nodded as he removed the beard from his chin. "It's in the case over there." He gestured with a free hand. "I'm a man of my word, like I said." He cared little for the money; it was worthless to him.

"I still don't understand why you needed to talk to that woman like that, feed her that bogus story about aging and auras and chakras and crap," the man said, as he jumped from the cot and moved over to the briefcase. He picked it up and shook it with determination before asking, "What's the code?"

"Same as last time: twenty fifty-nine," The mystic said before thinking, *The year of my birth.*

The now much younger looking mystic watched as the man began to count the money. He quickly slipped out the back flap of the tent and moved though the fairground, a long shadow walking beside him caused by the dangling overhead lights.

He came to the familiar tree behind the bumper car arena and looked over his shoulder to ensure no one was looking. He grabbed a small cube from his pocket and indented a series of buttons that littered the device. Satisfied with the imprints, he tossed the object into the swaying grass. The top of the cube burst open and the all-too-familiar shimmering of the black portal appeared. The mystic took one last deep breath of the closing summer air and snapped his eyes shut as he stepped forward.

When he opened his eyes an instant later, gone were the

blues and reds of the carnival, replaced with the dreary chrome and white of the transport room he had seen too many times to count.

Martin, his advisor, moved from behind a console and accepted the prosthetic beard from the mystic's outstretched hand. He smiled in congratulations, saying, "I saw everything, Brett. Very convincing performance. No anomalies detected." He paused. "I'm glad you tried the disguise this time and the story. She bought it. Deleting an anomaly-ridden reality is nasty work, not to mention the figurative paper pile that stems from it."

Brett nodded as he removed the aged wrinkle prosthetics and handed them to Martin as well. "Yes, she believed the story. But I still almost broke down again." He hung his head, his fingers pulling at the blue mystic outfit he still wore. "But I thought about how this was my last chance to … well, to keep my promise. That's what calmed me."

Martin clicked his tongue. "It wasn't your last chance. I could have lent you more money, you know that."

"No, I owe too much as it is—" Brett started, but Martin cut him off as he pointed at the blue robe, indicating it was time to remove it.

"The less time the props are out of quarantine, the better. The amount of work it would take to neutralise an anomaly in our prime reality…" Martin shuddered. "I hate to think of it. It has been years since I had to deal with one, and every year they just add more and more red tape and forms and signatures and statements."

Brett began to walk to the door of the time chamber and Martin followed him in a hurried fashion, his hand flying across a device he retrieved from his pocket. "Yup, reality tri-four, seven six, two echo is a healthy one. No need for clean-up of anything."

Brett let out a short breath in relief. "Good. I couldn't afford it anyway."

Martin gestured to the left hall where one of many prop

ROBERT J. BRADSHAW

rooms waited. Brett moved down the hall and took the third door on the left labelled: Early Millennium Clothing, 2050-2080. Martin followed him inside, his eyes still dancing around the screen of his device.

Brett walked up to the woman who stood behind the counter. "I'll be returning all of this." He gestured to himself and the items Martin held in his free hand.

"Will they need the standard cleaning package or advanced wash and repair?"

"Standard cleaning. I didn't fall or anything. Not like last time," Brett said, recalling the nasty rip that had occurred on the side of the outfit. That bloodstain had cost him dearly.

The woman checked something off on her terminal before looking to Martin. "It's been added to his account."

Martin nodded before placed the prosthetics on the table. He looked to Brett and said, "Get changed. There's something I need to ask you before we go our separate ways."

---

Brett sat down in front of Martin's bright white desk. He tried to hide how impressed he was by stroking his chin, but he couldn't help but admire the Lowevine Plastic furniture that littered the office.

Brett popped a caffeinated gum tab into his mouth and said, "I suppose guys like me helped you get such a big workspace."

Martin nodded. "Yes, but if you saw the work I had to do on the back end… Almost twelve-hour days most weeks."

Brett whistled. "I haven't had to work a double like that since I was a teenager."

"Yes, well, the reason I called you here is for an exit interview and to explain some of the plans we offer."

Brett chewed his gum and smiled slyly. "You mean try to sell me some more stuff."

Martin waved his hand. "Please, you'll want to hear about these options. The price is well worth it."

Brett settled into the padded back of the chair. "Go on, but you know I'm almost out of money."

Martin waved his hand again. "A payment plan can be arranged. Plus, these things would take place in the future once you've regained some of your wealth."

"Go ahead, tell me about the additional packages then."

"The 'Thanksgiving Visit' is a popular one with people in a similar situation as you and—"

"Not interested."

"But you don't even know what it is."

"I can figure."

Martin frowned. "Fine. The 'Christmas Day'— Let me finish," Martin continued as Brett opened his mouth to speak. "We supply you with the best camouflage technology to date. The same stuff the Ground Forces used on the Percious Belt Conflict. At a great price too. The deals really start to come in the more you agree to. Three consecutive Christmases and you'll see the savings." He paused, leaning back in his chair. "Want to relive a certain one, or maybe watch one from when you were a baby, or even one your parents were at before you came into the picture. All possible..." Martin trailed off as he could see Brett was staring past him.

Brett corrected his gaze as the lull in the conversation grew. "Look, I appreciate all your guidance and all the work you've done for me, but I'm just not interested. I did what I needed to do."

Martin typed something into his terminal before running a hand through his well-groomed sideburns. "And what was that exactly? It will help me close out the file."

"Have at least one reality where I'm not an orphan. Where I get to grow up with my mother in my life."

"Oh, yes," Martin said absently. "I remember now." He was clearly scrolling through his files.

"I did what I promised myself I would do all those years ago. I brought her back. Not for me, but for another version of myself."

"And wouldn't you like to visit that version of yourself? Interview him, or talk to your mother in that branch of the reality tree?"

Brett shook his head. "That's not why I did this. Money or not, I just wanted one of me to have a mother survive past that terrible day in August."

"Well, if I can't convince you, that's fine. No pressure at all. Just know the deal expires three months from now. If you decide after that to purchase a plan—"

"I know, I pay full price," Brett said as he looked to the tablet that sat in front of him, containing a six-question questionnaire.

He answered "Extremely Satisfied" for each question and stood, thanking Martin one last time before leaving the office.

As he moved down the hallway towards the elevator, he felt an odd sensation move up his spine. An image appeared to him then. It was a young Brett on that tragic day in August, except it wasn't so terrible now, as it had no reason to be. This child version of himself ran up and hugged his mother as she returned from work. The boy was smiling, looking past his mother, seemingly to the older Brett of the present.

Somewhere in all the realities that existed, Brett was no longer alone.

# SOUL KITCHENS

The band played on, and they played loud. Their swirling jazz orchestra notes roamed around the grandiose dining hall. The ladies and gentlemen in the audience sat at small circular tables, chatting and schmoozing and rolling with laughter as they conversed with one another. They drank their wines and sipped their whiskeys. Ate hearty meals and smoked with glee. The air was heavy above them, but quickly dissipated up into the bright plaster ceiling without issue or annoyance.

All the while, the soul kitchens were busy behind them.

"How many does that make today?" Edgar, a gentleman in his most brilliant tuxedo, asked as he sat at a table across from a happily married couple.

"Oh, a hundred thousand or so I would say," Gabriel replied as he turned away from the band and looked across the table. "Kitchen is a bit slow today, don't you think?" he added with a puff of grey smoke.

His wife, Cindy, who sat beside him, kissed his cheek took a sip of her bubbly before saying, "I think they're making them better these days. Better than they used to."

"Plus," Edgar continued, "it isn't easy work, no sir." The ice in his drink clinked against the glass as he raised the crystal container to his lips.

"Our job isn't easy either, for that matter," Gabriel replied, as he tried to navigate around Edgar's choice of words. His phrasing was rather forceful, but he held it behind a jovial smile. "We have to care for them, do we not?"

Cindy emitted a quick little laugh before saying, "I've been looking after six of them for a while now and one of them lives dangerously. Quite so indeed." She added a firm nod to reinforce her statement. Her cigarette holder bobbed in her gloved hand as she did so.

"Six?" Edgar chortled. "My word! I have three, and I must say, I do not agree with your assessment that they're making them better than they used to. No, I think they are using the same mold they used back in yesteryear. Remember those days, Gabriel?"

"Oh yes," Gabriel replied, as his vision returned to the band. His mind was elsewhere, thinking of contracts long finished.

"Well maybe it is I that has changed?" Cindy said before sipping her champagne.

Gabriel rubbed his hand against her back. "Well, you are a fair bit older than I," he said, before giving off a quick laugh.

Cindy gasped, hitting his hand in playful scorn. "Never remind a lady of her age!"

"It's those rough and tumble ones they have him looking after," Edgar said, pulling a box of matches from his jacket pocket. "That's where he gets it from, you know." He offered a sly smile to Gabriel before adding, "He was telling me all about them earlier on."

Gabriel shrugged as he watched Edgar light a new cigar. Hoping to avoid a lull in the conversation and the dangers that it would likely bring, he said, "Possibly. Quite possibly." Then he clapped his hands together as the band finished their song. "Marvelous music," he added, taking a hurried sip of his drink.

A whoosh from the kitchen was followed by a tinkling of bells down the hall.

Edgar craned his neck and looked over his shoulder towards the opening that served as a window into the kitchens. "There goes another one."

A lady in a smart black dress stood up at the next table over. She flattened her outfit against her legs and exited the dining hall. Her chocolate mousse was left half finished, the spoon sliding to the bottom of the bowl in its abandonment.

The band began to play again as Cindy took her eyes off the woman, saying, "Another one? She's over-worked as it is, poor thing."

Another whoosh and another bell.

"Two in a row," Edgar said, as he puffed on his cigar. "They're on a roll." His face held a smile, but Gabriel could detect the true meaning behind his words.

A gentleman with a top hat and a walking stick rose from his seat near the front of the hall. The cello player of the band saluted as the old timer headed towards the exit.

"Well, that one isn't going to last long," Edgar said as he watched his colleague move past the felt-covered doors.

"I'll say," Gabriel replied, leaning back in his chair. "That bloke's track record is terrible. He's lost a lot in his time. Most of them were easily avoidable."

Cindy clicked her tongue in distain. "Why don't they get rid of him? Send him to the gardens, tend to the flocks or serve in the courts?" she asked, a frown moving across her thin face.

"He's old, and he's got seniority," Edgar replied as he knocked the end of his cigar against the rim of the ashtray near the centre of the table.

"That doesn't make him good," Cindy replied with annoyance.

"I'll drink to that." Gabriel chortled and raised his glass, his eyes meeting Edgar's before his face disappeared behind the crystal.

After the three took a sip, Cindy added, "I heard he's been serving since they crossed the Rubicon."

The group laughed and drank, drank and laughed. Then a whoosh from the kitchen and the familiar toll of the bell.

"It's me," Cindy said, as she finished her drink in one gulp. "It's my turn." She rubbed her temples in a delicate fashion to sober up.

"No, say it isn't so," Gabriel said, downing his glass of whiskey. "The night is still young. You've already got six. Tell them upstairs—you've got too many."

"No, no. I can handle it," Cindy replied. "Besides, it will look good for my promotion interview coming up. Maybe I'll be your manager soon." She paused, a smile tugging at the corner of her lips. She leaned over and extinguished her cigarette in the ashtray. "But I won't have seven for long; I should be down to six by rotation's end."

"Oh?" Edgar exclaimed, sitting forward in his chair. "Is it the old fellow with the bad ticker?" A puff of smoke escaped from his mouth as he spoke.

"No, not him. One of the lost sheep, I'm afraid." Cindy said as she stood and adjusted her silver flapper headband. "It's time to shelter this young one from the world." She paused, swaying to the sounds of the music for a moment before adding, "The mother's nice, but the father? Well, I have my work cut out for me."

She left the table and the band played on. A whoosh and a bell followed soon after.

Edgar sat forward in his chair, flicking ash into the tray. "I heard that eight is going to become the new standard soon." He picked up his fork and began to gather the remainder of his meal on the end of it. "I didn't want to say anything to aggravate your missus."

"And how would you know that?" Gabriel asked as he tapped the side of his glass. It immediately filled with an auburn-coloured liquid.

"I have my sources," Edgar replied, a serious aura surrounded him.

Gabriel lifted the glass and swirled the liquid for several moments before replying, "Why? Does the boss think something bad is coming?"

His eyes drifted to several couples who occupied the dance floor in front of the band. He missed the time when Cindy had been less occupied with work.

"Oh yes. A storm approaches, I'm afraid." Edgar leaned back in his char. "The boss is sure of it. I heard from the son when he returned from his second attempt to change the course. But… well, you know how stubborn the children can be."

"I must agree with Cindy. I still say they are getting better."

Another whoosh, and another bell.

"Oh shoot, that's me," Gabriel said, looking to the kitchen. He blinked several times before standing up in a hurried fashion.

Edgar's face soured. "Oh, I was hoping we had more time. I wanted to get something off my chest."

Gabriel looked to his pocket watch. He had been hoping to avoid this conversation. "I suppose I have a minute. Healthy parents, both responsible, so I shouldn't be needed for a few more ticks of the hand," he said before returning to his seat.

Edgar sighed. "I… Well, to say you are the one I trust the most, I'll just come out and say it. I know why I'm constantly being left behind with no new assignments. It's because of him."

Gabriel sipped his drink to mask his concerned facial expression. He knew exactly who Edgar was alluding to. Some had called the child he had been assigned "a bad seed," others, "a lost cause." But these names were just kind descriptions for what that soul in particular had been…

A killer.

"I'm not sure what—" Gabriel started to say before Edgar shook his head, cutting him off.

"I tried my best with him. I tried to keep him on the straight and narrow. What hurts the most is, while you know what they

47

are doing is wrong, you've been with this child for their entire life. Seen everything they have seen. Understand the hand they've been dealt better than they do. We are ordered to get attached, to help them as much as we can, and I did those things." He paused, his eyes moving to his nearly empty drink. "Then I'm treated as a leper because of it. It bothers me that I was able to protect him while our colleagues failed to protect those he made his victims. I did my duty—nothing more, nothing less. I even did it when the retirement squads came for him, and I received the order from on high to stand down. My *duty*. That's all I've ever done."

"And no one is saying you didn't perform it to the best of your abilities." Gabriel paused, taking a moment to dab the sweat from his forehead with a handkerchief. "You are over-thinking this. You've had other assignments since then."

"No, you're mistaken. I'm still finishing with the ones I had on the go at the time. Here everyone is complaining about being overburdened and I'm the most underworked member of the protection service."

Gabriel chanced a look at his pocket watch, prompting Edgar to say, "Go ahead, leave me too. Everyone else has."

"No, no. I can stay. Still a few ticks until the birth. The mother is being responsible, and the father is a good driver."

"I just don't understand the distinction really. All of the children do harm, do bad things—but yet no one else is ostracised. It's just because I was good at my job and made them all look bad." Edgar paused, glancing to the ceiling.

Gabriel's eyes wandered to the nearby tables. He could tell that others were eavesdropping on their conversation.

Edgar lowered his head and continued, "But I'm hardly the first. All of those that had contracts like this, they've experienced the same cold shoulder that I have. But they also have another thing in common."

"What's that?" Gabriel asked, his peripherals on the second hand of his pocket watch.

"They all got transferred soon after." Edgar took a sip of his drink before adding, "When I came forth and rose through the ranks, I wanted nothing more than to be assigned to protection duties. It had everything—the glamour, the bragging rights. The difference one can make down there is almost incalculable. But here I am now, a disgrace."

"You're not though. Everyone understands. Like you said, this has happened before and will continue to happen for as long as the children are allowed to be as they are."

"I appreciate it, but your words aren't really helping." Edgar looked to his empty drink, defeated.

Gabriel felt a pit form in his chest. He worried for his friend, but as the seconds on the watch continued to tick by, he knew he needed to go. He stood slowly. "I'm sorry, I can't stay any longer." His tone revealed his sympathy. "The delivery doctor is good, and so are the nurses, but I can't miss this. You know what the boss says about those who miss the birth."

"I know, I know," Edgar said, extinguishing his cigar in the ashtray in front of him, his head turning to face the band.

Gabriel gave a soft smile in Edgar's direction before buttoning up his dinner jacket and pivoting. As he took a step towards the exit, he heard a woosh, followed by another bell.

Edgar's voice came up from behind. "Wait up, old chap. That's me!" The excitement in his voice was clear.

Gabriel slowed his pace and said over his shoulder, "That's great news. See, your worry was all for naught. You've got a new assignment."

Edgar pulled another cigar from his jacket pocket as he caught up to Gabriel. As the two exited the banquet hall, Edgar's face hardened before saying, "It won't last long. Too many defects; drug dependency will already be there at birth. See, I'm no good. Can't get anyone with promise anymore."

Gabriel shut his eyes tight. He knew Edgar was right in everything he was saying. He would never admit it, but he had heard a rumor too. *He's due to be transferred to kitchen duty any day now,* Gabriel thought as he vanished, appearing in the maternity ward of a hospital on the other side.

He put Edgar from his mind as he worked with several of his coworkers to ensure the baby was delivered without issue. Once the labour was over, the child was wrapped in a blanket and handed to the exhausted mother.

Gabriel looked into the infant's eyes. He couldn't explain it, but he detected something dark in them. He raised his head and looked out of the hospital windows and to the skyline beyond. His conversation with Edgar clung to the forefront of his mind.

# OF WINTER WINDS AND MIDLIFE CRISES

Harold followed in Becky's small footsteps as she ran ahead in the Martian snows.

"Look, Daddy. Look at it all!" she called back over the howling wind that engulfed the surrounding homes in a white powder.

"I see it, honey," Harold said as he tugged at the zipper of his coat, feeling the chill nip at his exposed neck. He wished he had listened to Teressa's advice and worn the scarf she had made.

"Daddy, look!" Becky called back, pointing to a snowman that sat in the field ahead. His daughter jumped up and down with excitement, before wading as quickly as she could through the knee-high snow over to the jolly creation.

*What a perfect day,* Harold thought, taking a deep breath. *The only thing that would make it better is a hot cup of coffee while I sit in front of the fire to warm up. Maybe crack open the book Teressa got me.*

He watched as his daughter jumped up to touch the snowman's head.

"Can we build a snowman? Just as big. No! Bigger!" Becky called. Her small voice was hardly audible over the rip-roaring winds that tore across the boulevard.

"Later, honey," Harold replied before looking over his shoulder, his eyes moving between the streetlights that served as markers back to their cozy house a short walk away. "Closer to the house," he added, upon facing forward once more.

"Okay," Becky answered as she poked the snowman in the stomach, the sound of disappointment hanging in her voice. She turned and ran in the direction of her father.

*What a relaxing day. Wonderful,* he thought, smiling to himself as he watched little Becky slowly return to the icy sidewalk he stood on. *Always loved the sound of snow as it falls. The still and calm of it all. So peaceful.*

But despite it all, he could feel the notion of returning to work the next day tugging at his mind.

He watched as Becky paused before diving into a pile of snow and laughing. In an attempt to clear his mind of the inevitable return to the office, he thought, *It has been a great week. Nothing better than having time off around the holidays. Nothing.* Harold smiled at the sky. *December twenty-fifth, World Peace Day. Best holiday of the year.*

Becky made a snowball and threw it towards the snowman. The compacted snow fell well short, but was still an impressive throw for a child who had celebrated her sixth birthday only a few weeks prior.

Harold looked at his watch, the crystalline digital blue numbers showing a time of quarter to eleven. He looked up. "Becky, honey, time to head back."

"Aw, but you said—"

"I said back at home by ten forty. It's past that," Harold replied in a calm, yet authoritative voice.

"Five more minutes," Becky wined, and picked up another wad of snow.

"Breakfast is going to be ready soon."

He watched as his daughter dropped the unfinished snowball and preceded to dive into an adjacent pile of snow to make a snow angel. Her pink snowsuit shone bright in contrast to the constant white that surrounded her.

Harold looked to the grey sky and felt the snowflakes melt on the warmth of his face. He returned his gaze downward as he saw Becky stand carefully from her creation. She took several deliberate steps to exit it as to not tarnish what she had made.

"It's beautiful, honey. No more though; we have to eat. You can play after."

Hearing this, Becky slumped over and hung her arms at her sides.

"I know, life's tough," Harold added as he watched Becky slowly walk over. "Bet there's pancakes inside."

"Pancakes!" Becky cheered. In an instant she was standing tall, marching towards the streetlamps that pointed in the direction of home.

———

"Boots," Harold reminded his daughter as he opened the door to their house.

Becky ran inside, stopping just short of the point where tile met carpet and sitting on the steps that led up to the bedrooms, tearing off the Velcro straps of her boots. She picked them up and tossed them over the vent.

"Mommy, we saw a snowman!" Becky called through the house as she ran to the kitchen.

"That's lovely, dear," Teressa's voice drifted from around the corner. The smell of bacon wafted from the kitchen.

Harold stomped his boots on the snow receiver before untying them and placing them beside his daughter's over the vent. Then he removed his coat, placing it on a hanger in the open closet.

He blinked in self-reflection as his hands left the jacket. He realised that it was highly probable that the next time he would be needing his coat would be early tomorrow morning for his commute to work.

He walked into the kitchen and watched as Teressa stood over the stove, spatula in hand, her long brunette hair twisted into a bun as a pancake sizzled in front of her.

"Good walk, hun?" she asked, before flipping the pancake over.

"Really good. Cleared my head a bit. Becky had the most fun though, isn't that right?" He looked to Becky, who gave an exaggerated nod as she sipped a glass of orange juice that had been left out for her.

"That's wonderful," Teressa replied as she removed a trio of sizzling bacon strips from a second pan. She paused as she placed the bacon in a bowl and covered it with a plate. "I can't believe you have to go to work tomorrow. The day after World Peace Day."

Harold let out a slight chuckle as he sat down across from his daughter. He had been thinking about that since his eyes had first opened that morning. In an attempt to be more positive, he replied, "I've had a whole week off already. I guess you like having me around the house?"

Teressa smiled and nodded. "Of course, I do. I never see you, it seems." She added some uncooked bacon to the pan and the kitchen was filled with the sounds of sizzling grease. "Last year you had the day after the holiday off. Why not this year?"

Harold poured himself a glass of orange juice as he said, "Mr. Shaw is very excited about the project I proposed before the vacation. Very excited." He heard the hint of distance in his voice and took a sip from the glass before adding, "If this project goes well and the factory can mass produce them, that will finally give us the money we need to move into the mountain high-rises. Just like you always wanted to. Live up there with the mountaineers overlooking the entire valley."

"I do like it here," Teressa replied.

"I do too," Becky added with gusto. "I never want to move. Never, ever."

"But the mountains, honey. Think of them. Being able to see far off. Remember what it looked like when we hiked in the summer? The reds and yellows and blues. Gorgeous."

Teressa nodded in acquiescence.

"Daddy, you said after leaving Earth, we would never move again."

Teressa turned and tilted her head as if to say, "You did say that."

"I'm surprised you remember that," Harold replied as he got up and headed to the coffee maker. "You weren't even four yet."

"I remember!" Becky nodded enthusiastically. "You took us to the beach at our old house. You said heading to Mars was our one move and that we would have so much fun. See, I remember." Becky nodded again after her statement, showing how happy she was with her superior memory skills.

"I guess I did," Harold replied, attempting to remember the intricacies of the conversation, but failing to come up with anything substantial. He grabbed the now full cup of coffee from the dispenser. "But wouldn't you rather live in a bigger house with nothing but the sky above you, and the tops of the city below?"

"No," Becky said with sincerity as she kicked her dangling legs from the chair.

Harold shrugged and returned to his seat. He blew on his coffee and looked to his wife as she placed the fresh pancake on top of a mound. "Honey, you like it here right? On Mars?"

Teressa brought the plate over. "Of course, I do. I miss the nature sanctuaries back home and our quiet little city"—she kissed her husband on the temple—"but I like it here because you like it. I like that you like your job. I like that Mr. Shaw appreciates good employees. Honest, hardworking people like you. I think this move has worked out for us. Worked out for our family."

"I like it here," Becky said as she smiled at the plate of pancakes that appeared before her. I like the summer rains and the fall leaves and the winter snows and… And…" She trailed off as she speared a pancake like it was a fresh catch.

"The spring blossoms?" Teressa asked after a moment, placing a stack of pancakes on a second plate.

"Yes, the spring blo— blah—" Becky looked to the ceiling light as she struggled with the word, her chewing growing slower as she focused.

"Blossoms," Teressa repeated. "B-L-O-S-S-O-M-S. It's a big word."

"And you like your job here?" Harold asked, his voice calm.

"Sure." Teressa shrugged. "I mean, it's nothing I couldn't be doing anywhere, but I don't mind it. I like the people I'm with. More calm days than stressful days. Pay is okay. What more can I ask for?" She reached over to the dispenser and selected the tea option. A clean mug was forwarded from its base and a tea bag dropped into it from the overhang slot. "Why all these questions, Harold? Are you having a bit of a midlife crisis?"

"A bit early for that, don't you think? I'm thirty-two. I hope I live longer than sixty-four!" He shook his head. "I just wanted to make sure I made the right choice, you know?"

He went back into his memories, thinking about the stress of moving planets. He was worried at the time if he was making the right decision.

He cleared his throat, bringing himself back to the present, and looked at Becky. "You like your school and everything?"

Becky nodded as she shovelled a fork load of pancake towards her face.

Teressa put a hand on Harold's arm. "I think you're just stressed about the designs for the project and the presentation. Once it gets the go ahead from Mr. Shaw, you'll feel right as rain."

"You think so?"

"I know so. I think you just put too much pressure on yourself. Too much weight on living up on the mountains with the upper class. We like it here. Don't feel we have to move based on us, because we don't have to." She paused, cutting her stack of pancakes before adding, "Plus, having to pack up everything again, reorganise all our belongings, hire the movers... It's just a pain."

"You're right as usual," Harold said as he slowly added some butter substitute to his food. "But I wonder, if Mr. Shaw and the board don't like the project, I—"

"First off," Teressa said, rubbing his arm, "don't think like that. And secondly, if he doesn't like it, you always have your backup plan."

"And that is?" Harold asked, looking into his wife's brown eyes.

"You join Fred's mining company. You know he would take you in a second. He looks up to you."

Harold put down the utensils and sipped his coffee. "My brother can be a bit ... eccentric. Not to mention difficult to work with."

"So? He's your brother. You've dealt with him your whole life, and have you actually tried to work with him as equals on a project? His company isn't—"

"Mommy?" Becky said, as she played with the puddle of syrup that had submerged her last pancake.

"—Isn't that far. A thirty-minute commute from here and—"

"Mommy?" Becky asked again.

"—You enjoy the mining aspect, obviously you do. You take your designs and sell them to your brother and his company. He will love your idea for the new—"

"Mommy?"

"What, honey?" Teressa replied, finally relenting.

"What's eccentric mean?"

"Eccentric means ... difficult. Or strange," she replied, as she turned her head to face her husband. "So, you show him—"

"I like Uncle Fred," Becky added. "He always brings cake when he visits."

"Yes, he does." Teresa returned her gaze back to her husband and asked, "What was I saying?"

"The new mining laser—selling the design to Fred, if Mr. Shaw doesn't like it."

"Right. Um, right," Teressa replied, as she took a small bite of her breakfast. "But again, that's your backup plan, because Mr. Shaw will love it. You said it will save the company money in the long run and if your presentation shows that, then…" She trailed off, waiting for Harold to confirm what she had said.

"It does. I made that the central point." He pointed his fork at his wife as he said, "It wasn't easy. You know how much I hate presentations. Designing the stuff, no problem. But delivering a speech and selling the device to people? That's a different thing entirely. That's why salespeople are a necessary evil."

"Well, there you go," Teressa said, as she bobbed her teabag around her mug.

"There are always the rings of Saturn. That looks like a wild job," Harold said after a long lull in the conversation.

"Honey, what's going on? Why are you so … *listless*?"

"I don't know; I guess I'm just in a funk or something. I like work. I like Mars. I like our house. I just can't explain it. I'm not bored, but I'm not … stimulated." He shrugged. "I don't know. Forget about it. I'll just work through it."

"Well, you better not let this affect you tonight because you know your sister is taking the shuttle from the United Provinces and will here by six. And your brother is supposed to be here around the same time."

Harold nodded slowly, prompting Teressa to add, "That's the look of someone who'd forgotten."

"I didn't forget," Harold added quickly, though his defensive tone told Teressa all she had to know.

"Sure, but you know you could always mention the new laser design to your brother tonight, since he'll be here anyway.

See what he thinks. Maybe that's it—maybe you want to tell him, but feel too attached to your current work."

Harold poked at a pancake with his fork and said, "Yeah, maybe."

But while his lips moved, he thought, *I've thought about working for Fred for a while now. The pay would be less. A lot less. But maybe together we could build something out here for our family, something that would be ours. Not Shaw Industries' or the board's, but the Drysdale Family's. I could turn Fred's company into a real competitor with my designs. Then a few government contracts and we would be made.*

Harold sipped his coffee. "I already have a few ideas how I could improve his company. Better profit margins… He showed me his quarterly books last World Peace Day. I could help him."

Teressa chewed her food and offered a quick shrug in reply as if to say, "I know you could."

"Daddy," Becky said as she pushed her empty plate forward, "I finished my breakfast. Can we go outside again?"

"Sure, honey," Harold said with an absent smile. "Let's build that snowman."

---

"I'm telling you, Harry. Seriously, come work with me," Fred said in his usual jovial manner. "Out there on the perimeter. Digging away. More technology with us in our company trucks than the first Martian rockets had in all their colony ships. Getting down—*way down*—into the surface."

"Sounds dangerous. I've always said that," Melissa said, looking between her two younger brothers.

Fred looked to his sister and said, "Dangerous? Nothing worth doing hasn't been dangerous. Discovery of atomic drives? Dangerous. Colonizing the moons? *Really* dangerous. The renewable quantum fields? You bet your butt that was dangerous. But look where we are with all of these advancements."

"I suppose," Melissa said as she swirled the wine around in her glass.

"We just got a new contract, Harry. Biggest yet," Fred said as he admired the stubby whiskey glass in his hand. "Big stuff. Adventure. Gotta open up a new shop; it's too far to drive from the current one. Work Monday to Wednesday—long days—then an easy day on Thursday followed by the drive home, so it's a full week." He gave a quick laugh again. "Have you home to the wife and kids by eight at night. Just in time for the new release data uploads."

"I like that," Teressa said, as she walked out of the kitchen with a fresh glass of wine. "But Harold likes his current job, right, darling?"

"Um, right," he answered. He had hardly heard her as he was hanging off every word his brother had said. "How many people for this new contract you think?" Harold asked, as he raised his drink to his lips.

"Oh, full crew; twenty-six people. But I ain't got that many to spare. Most of my people will be at Tampareen Post. So I'm going to have to hire." He sipped his drink, savouring the flavour before adding, "Did I mention we're hiring?" He turned his head. "Teressa, do you want a job? You're good at the math stuff."

"No, thank you," Teressa replied, in a sing-song way. "Stuck in a cabin with a bunch of smelly guys. Muddy and dirty and—"

"But you love nature. And you can't be more in nature than surrounded by it," Fred quickly retorted. "And it's not all guys. I've got lots of woman in my employ, you know. Like Emily, Sarleen, Ashley, um…"

"Run out of names already?" Melissa asked with a teasing grin on her face.

"Not quite," Fred replied quickly as he took another sip, a searching look on his face.

Teressa gave a polite smile before standing. Becky had come from the other room and gestured her mother over.

"Why didn't you ask me?" Melissa asked as she adjusted her long red hair behind her back.

"You just finished saying how dangerous it is." Fred replied.

Melissa shrugged, leaning against the arm of the sofa.

Fred continued, "Besides I thought if Teressa worked for me that would convince Harry to jump ship and come work for a company that cares. One that carries his father's last name." He looked to his brother and added, "There is nothing I would like more than for my brother to come work for me."

Teressa returned to her spot beside Harold and nudged his arm. Harold flinched at the bump and said, "I'm flattered. Really, I am."

"Come on, get your hands dirty! I know sitting behind that desk—nice suit, white walls—is killing you. Come out where the sun is. The fresh air will do you some good." Fred nodded at his own words before adding, "Think about it: Harold Drysdale, vice president, Drysdale Mining Limited. I quite like the sound of that."

Harold leaned forward and finished off his whiskey. "I like the sound of that too."

Fred turned to his sister and smiled. "I think I've been getting to him."

"Well, I'm going to have another drink," Harold said as he stood. "Anyone else want anything while I'm up?"

"I'll take another one," Fred said as he took a handful of cashews from the bowl on the table in front of him. "Some of us have tomorrow off," he added with a quick wink to Harold.

"I'll come with you," Teressa offered, looking to her husband. "I could use a top up of wine."

Melissa nodded. "I'm coming too."

The three headed to the kitchen, leaving Fred to watch the artificial fireplace. Harold poured two glasses of whisky as Melissa said, "He really wants you to work for him, you know. He's always looked up to his big brother."

"I know, I know," Harold replied, placing the cap back on the bottle. "I should work for him."

"I know you're giving it thought; you're letting him actually get a word in about it this year," Teressa added as she grabbed the wine bottle from beside him. "Last year you shot him down pretty quickly."

Harold shrugged. "What can I say? He makes some good points. I do miss the hard work, and the feeling of real job satisfaction." Harold rubbed his fingers together to give texture to his words. "A real job well done, you know?"

"You know Dad would be happy to hear it. He loves when his boys get along." Melissa nodded in thanks as Teressa finished topping off the wine glasses. Turning back to the living room, she added, "Well, think about it at least."

Teressa and Harold stood alone in the kitchen. The sound of Becky's cartoons playing from upstairs echoed down the hall.

"What are you thinking?" Teressa asked. "I can see the wheels in your head turning."

Harold swished the ice around in his glass. "I'm thinking if I work with Freddy that I would only see you guys on the weekends. I would be away from home a lot."

Teressa chuckled. "So how it is now, then?" She put a hand on his back and kissed him. "Honey, you do a lot of hours at work as it is."

Harold took another sip. In those brief seconds he thought about his last few months at work, and the listless feeling he had been having. The need for something new. Something bold. Something adventurous. An opportunity he had been yearning for was currently knocking on his door at this very instant.

He adjusted his gaze and looked deep into his wife's eyes as he said, "I'm going to do it. I'm going to tell him about the new laser designs."

---

The snowy landscape flecked off Harold's ski-goggles as he sat on a fallen log, studying the winter plains. He could see his breath moving though the mask he wore as he looked at the untamed frontier before him. The white of the snow twisted this way and that in the wind, and the growing treeline in the distance had become a series of odd shapes as the weight of the snow burdened the branches they lay upon. He held a thermos of coffee in his hand and felt completely at peace.

Harold heard the crunching of snow behind him and could tell by the cadence of the steps that it was Fred approaching.

"I like to look at it sometimes, too," Fred said as he moved up beside his brother and nodded at the frontier. "I've never been in this quadrant before, but the frontier is the frontier. 'Tough country' is the term the old pioneers of Earth would have used." He paused. "I read that once and it has always stuck with me."

Harold nodded and unscrewed his thermos. He knew his brother was using the term incorrectly, but didn't want to correct him in the moment. "Yup, it's something to look at."

Fred turned and brushed off the snow on the spot beside Harold. He sat down, grunting as he did so. "Well, how was your first full week with us?"

Harold turned and looked into his brother's ski goggles, seeing his own reflection in them. "It was hard work. But I think it's just what I need. I haven't slept this well since before Becky was born."

Fred slapped him on the back. "That's good to hear. Truly, I'm happy to hear that. You were wasted at that old job of yours. Just a number. A cubie. Out here though, you ain't no number; you're my brother, and a true help to this team. Once we get your prototype back from the fabricators, oh, do I have high hopes for the device."

Harold watched as the snow began to build on Fred's jacket as he moved his face covering out of the way to sip his coffee. "I just wish I had done this sooner. The only thing holding me back was my loyalty to the company. A couple years at a place and you build a certain level of loyalty."

"You build familiarity," Fred said, pulling the zipper of his jacket higher. "Two completely different things."

"I guess—" Harold started.

"But you said Shaw didn't even mind," Fred interrupted as he looked out to the swirling plains ahead.

"I said that he wasn't as upset as I thought he would be. He didn't even mention my outstanding projects. He accepted the notice and only wanted to ensure I finished my contributions to the Laskey Project and passed any other work to Reet. Which I did."

"See? Just a number there."

Harold sat for a while as Fred's words tumbled through his mind. He took several sips of his coffee. He felt a twinge in his back each time he hoisted the thermos to and from his mouth. The week's labour had been eager to unveil muscles he didn't even know existed.

"Thank you for having me here, Freddy," he said after several moments. "I really appreciate it. I've been so listless lately. I needed a change."

Fred put his arm around his older brother's shoulders. "I know. I've been there too."

"You have?" Harold asked, sealing his thermos and feeling the heat of the liquid move around his torso.

"Ya, but not a midlife crisis—what they call a quarter life crisis. I was twenty-two. That's when I left the heating and cooling job."

"One of the last trades still unionised. Mom was so upset, I remember."

"And I understood. But I could feel myself wasting away there, and one day I thought, *If you're still working here in twenty years, you'll hate yourself.* I needed to be my own person. Run the show. Dad called that vain, but I knew what I needed, and I went for it."

"Well…" Harold started to say before emitting a quick laugh. "He doesn't think you're vain anymore. He tells everyone about his son the business owner."

Fred laughed. "Funny how success changes people's opinions of you." He brushed the snow off his thermal pants. "But I can't blame the guy. I took a risk, just like you did by coming out here. Two crises, just at different points in our lives. And we are both happier for it."

"Cheers to that," Harold said, hoisting his thermos.

"Cheers to that," Fred repeated and pulled a small thermos of his own from his jacket pocket.

They clinked the containers together before Harold asked, "Should we get back and help pack up the trucks?"

Fred's mask shifted and Harold knew he was smirking under it. "Always were the slave driver," he said with a laugh. He returned the thermos to his pocket before adding, "I guess we've got to get you home. You'll have to tell Teressa all about your first week in person."

Harold stood as well, pushing his face covering back up to his ski goggles. "I already called her a few times from the temp house. I know Becky has been dying to see me; apparently she has lots of questions. Oh, and she wants to know if you'll visit more now that we're working together."

"I'll see what I can do. I'm about to get a lot busier at home," Fred said as they moved towards the temporary encampment they had built several dozen metres away.

Harold knew that by staying silent Fred would spill whatever occupied his mind. After several paces his younger brother did just that.

"I've been meaning to tell you for a few months now: Heather's pregnant. We were saving the news for—"

Harold turned and hugged his brother. "That's great news! When we get back to the city come inside and have a drink with me to celebrate."

"My news? Or that you had a successful first week?" Fred asked, as he patted his brother on the back.

"Why not both?" Harold replied as released his brother from the embrace. He felt a tear form in his eye as he knew he had made the right choice by accepting Fred's offer to work for him. For the first time in his life, he was no longer stuck in the perpetual wheel of chasing something. He was at peace.

# YOU DID THIS

"It is confirmed, sir," General Harland said as he leaned forward in his chair. He pointed at the display screen at the head of the briefing table. "Despite their defensive matrix, we managed to figure out the code."

The general nodded to someone at the back of the room, but I kept my eyes forward, glued to the screen. The display changed from Luna's distant silhouette to a close-up view of the Zelstra Peninsula. The image was clear.

Missile sites, at various stages of construction.

Harland let out a sigh. "It's irrefutable."

"Do they know that we know?" Admiral Krellic asked as she pointed to the screen. "Do they know that we've cracked their mirage shroud?"

"Not as of this second, but once they see our response, they will figure it out pretty quickly," General Harland replied, a look of amusement flashing across his face.

I glanced between the two officers, my thoughts turning to why Admiral Krellic seemed so surprised by this information. *Surely she should have been briefed beforehand? She's the chief officer of the navy.* But as my eyes lingered on Harland's coy smile, the answer became obvious. *He wanted himself and his ground force intelligence to receive the credit for the find.*

"I warned you, Mr. Chairman," a voice to the right of me said, jarring me from my thoughts. Upon hearing my title, I looked down the table to my minister of system affairs. "I warned you at the time that if we let the moon fall to that government referendum, they would join the Mons government."

I opened my mouth to counter when Admiral Krellic added, "I agree. This problem should have been handled a decade ago. Then we would not be in this situation."

I felt the thundering of my pulse in my neck. I took a short breath before saying, "Don't sit here and judge me for that decision. I wasn't prepared to invade a neutral entity over the fact that they were holding a goddamned election. For exercising their right to freedom. Isn't that what our government is supposed to support?" I laid my hands flat on the table. "The death toll... No one remembers that part, do they?"

I paused, my mind turning to the various briefings I had received about the manifesto the politicians of Mars liked to cite. "Not to mention the possibility of the Mons government deciding to cite their honour code as a means to intervene. That was a very real possibility."

I could tell by the blank expressions on the faces around me that the details I was mentioning had long jettisoned from the grey matter of their minds. "Part of their sphere of influence? Does that ring any bells?" I prompted.

Harland glanced down at the table before looking to me. He clearly thought my little outburst was beneath a man of my position.

"I agree. We cannot live in the past. We need to focus on the here and now." Harland's index finger drove into the table at the utterance of the final word. "We need to take out those missiles before they become operational."

I held up a hand in a defensive gesture. "Wait, wait, wait.

You're talking about invading, aren't you, David?" My eyes were locked on his clean-shaven face. "In so many words, that's what you're saying. That's where this is headed?"

As I spoke aloud my inner voice was working overtime. *Change the damn record already; I've heard this one.*

Harland laid his palms flat on the table. "In so many words? Yes." I recoiled in horror, prompting him to quickly add, "Sir, this is the only option. Our usual approaches—hacking, data blinders, bribes—none of that solves the problem. And to be honest, I doubt it would even shut them down."

There was a disturbance near the end of the table, prompting me to look down to Harvey Wells, my minister of economic harmonies. As all eyes turned to him, he said, "I'm sorry, I just don't understand. Why is there such a big response to this? The Martian state has had missiles since before the separation. Defensive satellites, rail gun platforms, all—"

Admiral Krellic rolled her eyes before saying, "Exactly, *defensive* is the primary word."

"They never had first strike capability," Harland added, finishing the admiral's sentence. "Those missiles they launch from Mars would give us weeks of warning and we could intercept them. Missiles shot from the moon? We would have minutes."

Harvey's mouth hung open for a moment before his gaze gravitated over to me. "It's clear, Jason. We have to act."

I shut my eyes tight as his words stung me. If Harvey was with them, then what choice did I have? I was hoping he would have been the one to talk some sense into the military arm of my government.

I picked up the optical stylus in front of me and rubbed it between my fingers as I spoke. "You realise if we invade an entity affiliated with the Mons government, they will react."

Harland nodded at the unseen person to the back of the room and the image of the display changed to that of an orbital image of Luna. "We estimate they have four sites completed." The image shifted to show red circles appearing across the surface. "With two more nearly complete." Yellow circles appeared just south of the equator. "We also see they have another six in various stages of completion." He paused, before nodding to himself. "We can guarantee that our weapons can eliminate all of the sites."

"Guarantee?" I replied, my eyes narrowed with disbelief.

"Yes, sir. A few orbital strikes and those sites will be wiped from the map."

"And what about the people at those sites? The workers, soldiers, civilian personnel nearby? The Luna government will demand bloodshed in return."

Admiral Krellic chuckled. "Let them. They knew the cost of rejecting our olive branch and going into the open arms of Mars would be high." She paused, taking a long glance at the display. "And to answer your question, Mr. Chairman, if they launch anything that goes even a dozen metres off the surface, my people will destroy it immediately."

Harland nodded in agreement before adding, "That's where the politics comes in." He sounded almost resentful. "Obviously we don't want to have to annex the moon." He looked to an officer beside him who was pointing to something on a data pad. "We would be fighting a guerrilla war for the next three years and a minor insurgency for twenty. No, we need to reach out and tell them to accept our supplies and money. This will allow them to rebuild. Of course, we would get them to formally sign that damned arms contract that they have been so flippant about in return."

"They will refuse," I replied, my jaw tight.

"I'm not so sure they will. A million soldiers racing to the surface to capture the twin capitals will change their tune."

"They will see this as an unprovoked attack. Death of thousands will be the result. If it was the other way around, would you accept the money, the false sorrow?"

"I wouldn't have pointed missiles at the largest military force in known space," Harland added, his tone hardened.

"And what do we do when the Mons government retaliates?" I asked, looking around the table.

I was met with several blank faces before Admiral Krellic replied in a soft tone, "Sir, I think you are missing the point. Respectfully, they are building their missiles for war. They mean to strike first. We are doing this to save the lives of everyone on Earth. Every life on Mars, too, for that matter."

I opened my mouth to offer a retort but stopped myself. I hadn't thought of it like that. If Luna did fire her weapons, we would know the order originated from the Mons government and we would retaliate in kind. Firing our entire arsenal at both Mars and Luna. The idea that we were within range of Mons-affiliated weapons made us lose our advantage, and more importantly, made us feel vulnerable. The entire game had changed.

I realised that I had not spoken in a while when General Harland added, "But if the Luna government doesn't accept our proposition, then we annex it to ensure this can never happen again." He pointed at the screen when it changed from an orbital view of the northern capital. The shimmering of its artificial atmosphere gave the city a golden hue.

"We already have a battle plan drawn up." Harland looked down the table toward an officer whose name I had long forgotten and said, "Colonial Greyson and I conducted several war games last year. The strategy we are about to propose was overwhelmingly successful." His proud words moved past a gloating smile.

I heard the officer Harland had singled out thank his superior before making several comments about the strategy at hand, but I ignored them. My mind raced as I attempted to process everything I was hearing. My brain struggling to grapple with the reality of what war with the Mons government would entail.

*If Luna does not accept the proposal, the death toll will be measured in the millions.* I could feel the sweat pooling on my palms. *But that is only one possibility. If they do accept our offer and we bring them back to the fold, then the carnage will be limited to just the missile sites.*

I paused my train of thought as I heard Harland use several military buzzwords that caught my attention. But as the general continued, I quickly returned to my thought process.

*Like Admiral Krellic said, they knew what they were doing when they bult those sites. Only they did not expect to be caught. Didn't expect their mirage technology to compromised.*

"Would you like to see stage one of the proposed invasion strategy?" Harland asked, pulling me once again from my thoughts.

I ignored the question. "And we're sure Mons can't hit us? We are sure all our intel is correct? They still haven't cracked the slip drive tech?"

Minister Trusford of Mars public relations nodded. "All my people on the ground confirm they have always been met with dead ends..." He trailed off. I know he wanted to say something more, no doubt about sabotage efforts, but he had always kept his cards close to his chest.

Admiral Krellic added, "We've done daily scans since Luna went independent. There are no ships, satellites, orbital plat-forms—nothing from the Mons government we don't know about lurking in our space." She paused, uncrossing her arms to vaguely point towards the projection. "The few trade ships and diplomatic vessels that are currently in our zone would be rounded up and quarantined before the orbital bombardment begins to ensure they don't retaliate in some way."

General Harland grabbed a piece of lint from below the array of medals pinned to his chest. "Sir, I'll be blunt. I can guarantee that their missile sites will be decimated in a strike. I can also guarantee that this will be the most one-sided skirmish Sol has seen in three hundred years. But it only stays one sided if we act now. The more sites they build, the more arms they stockpile, the less of an advantage we have."

Admiral Krellic nodded emphatically. "I must agree with the general on this. The longer we wait, the higher the probability they figure out we have cracked their mirage systems. Once they realise that, there is not a doubt in my mind they will move their sites underground and we go back to square one."

I held up an impatient hand. "Underground? But couldn't that be the case now? Couldn't they have more sites that we can't see?"

Harland looked to a trio of officers beside him and all three shook their heads in unison. Harland returned his gaze to me as he responded, "They would have no need. They think they are still safe behind their mirage tech. Plus, the cost of constructing silos like that below the moon's surface? Frankly, that's out of their budget, even with the Mons government fronting them the money."

"Out of the budget until they realise they have no choice, that is," Krellic added, narrowing her eyes at Harland.

"Yes, of course," Harland verbally backpedaled.

I looked at the lunar surface, my eyes moving between the lights of the various sized cites, the two capitals on either pole.

My subconscious spoke again, *They're right, those missiles were put there to target us. To destroy our advantage. To put a stop to the peace that has existed for so many years. People will die, but are a few thousand now not better than potential billions once they launch those missiles?*

"Mr. Chairman?" General Harland prompted after a moment. "There is nothing else we can say at this point. I've already given you my guarantee, and I will add this: If we take out these sites, no civilians on Earth will die. Isn't that enough?"

I nodded slowly. The Luna and the Mons governments had put me in this situation with their blatant disregard for the peace treaties and their overconfidence in their mirage technology. I sighed. "The navy handles bombardment while the ground forces go in to secure the sites and prepare for annexing the capitals?"

Both senior officers nodded before Harland added, "They'll agree to the terms, you mark my words. You are making the right choice, sir."

I sat in the command control portion of the government complex. My eyes locked on Admiral Krellic as she nodded in satisfaction at the blips that moved about the screen at the head of the room.

"All Mons and Luna controlled transports ships in our space have been quarantined, their coms jammed." She turned around to face me. "Bombardment will begin within moments."

General Harland strolled past her, his hands clasped behind his back. "Excellent work, Admiral. I have the dropships on the U.E.S. Europa and U.E.S. Singapore set to launch the first wave of troops once our spotters report good effect on target." He chuckled. "The Luna sensors are going to be off the charts with this many blips in their skies."

"I've already told my corsair pilots to hit any site that fires at your people," Krellic replied as she tucked a loose strand of hair behind her ear. "You set 'em up and we'll knock 'em down."

I sat back in my chair and studied the various video feeds around the room. Our fleet of ships moved about slowly, still assigned to pre-established patrol routes as to not arouse suspicion. Once their guns opened up they would break routine and join a new formation.

I felt a sense of calm come over me as I listened to the cavalier banter of the senior officers around the room. I figured if they could be this relaxed before a major offensive than they must have complete faith in the mission and their people.

*Who am I to doubt them?*

"U.E.S. Gemini and Taurus have reached patrol marker Kilo,"

Admiral Krellic stated, her eyes fluttering to the main screen. "And right on cue, they've begun bombardment."

I watched as the main view screen shifted to a broadcast from the U.E.S. Taurus. A barrage of ordnance burst from its massive weapons and soared towards the distant Luna. Its guns adjusted a few degrees before firing another salvo.

In my peripheral I could see the smaller screens were broadcasting the feed from the U.E.S. Gemini. It showed a nearly identical picture.

"U.E.S. Viking has doubled back and is firing now as well," Krellic added, an air of excitement clinging to her voice.

General Harland grabbed a mug from the operation table. He took a sip of his coffee before pushing a finger against his earpiece. "Spotter control is sighting good kills across the board. All missile sites are confirmed destroyed."

"Roger that, General," Krellic said over her shoulder, before speaking into the microphone affixed to the collar of her jacket. "U.E.S. Singapore and U.E.S. Europa, move from secondary position and get into drop-off range." She moved her hand across her wrist-mounted device and added, "Time set at five minutes forty-two seconds until they are ready to drop off your forces." She made eye contact with General Harland. "Then it's your operation from here on…"

She trailed off, her eyes darting around the room.

I watched as General Harland pushed his earpiece deeper into his ear canal. "Repeat?" His mouth twitched after uttering the word.

Admiral Krellic moved her hands across the keyboard in front of her and muttered, "It can't be right. Must be phantom signals."

"What's happening?" I asked, looking around at the flurry of officers who stared at their terminals with dumbfounded expressions.

Harland spoke, but I could tell he was still listening to

reports from his earpiece. "We have multiple missile launch signatures…"

"From where? Mars or Luna?" I was standing now, my eyes locked on the screen that showed the U.E.S. Taurus. I saw no light flashes or blips on the targeting scope, just Luna's natural shimmer.

"No. Negative," Harland said before switching communicator channels on his wrist terminal. "Get me the commander of the defensive net. I want…" He moved to the far side of the command control room, and I could no longer decipher what he was saying over the clamouring voices.

"Admiral, please tell me what is going on. Did we miss a site?" I asked, my voice a pleading mess.

Admiral Krellic looked at the main viewscreen as it shifted to an orbital feed of Earth. A green grid overlayed the globe. I felt a chill move over me, as I could see hundreds of red lines moving towards targets all across the planet. Each signal originated from black nothingness.

"They couldn't have just come from nowhere," I said, my voice distant. "They don't have the drives for it."

Admiral Krellic spoke, her eyes never leaving the screen. "Stealth ships. It's gotta be. Better than anything we have."

"What? We ran daily patrols! You said we sweep our space constantly! How?"

I watched as more red lines sprang up. The missiles from these phantom ships now headed to secondary targets.

"They could have been there for months, maybe years, cycling out with replacement vessels," she added. Her voice broke as she repeated, "Better than anything we have."

I saw a timer appear on the bottom of the screen. We had less than two minutes until the first missiles hit their targets.

General Harland ran over to the Admiral and said, "Our defensive net coordinator is saying we don't have the capability for this. They are projecting they can only get twenty percent of the missiles. They don't have enough time to get them all." His eyes snapped to me. "Sir, give the order to retaliate. Targets on Mars and Luna are preassigned from the simulations. Just give the order."

I watched as several red lines vanished from the screen as our defensive net got to work. I noted that barely a dent was made against the sea of contacts racing towards the surface. I stood there in a stupor, understanding that all life on Earth would be extinguished in a matter of seconds.

"Sir, we don't have time!" Harland shouted. "I need the order."

"Fire our missiles," I replied, hardly realising I had done so.

General Harland spun around and began shouting the orders into his earpiece. He took two paces away and I felt everything slow down to a crawl. My eyes moved to the screen as the display shifted to show thousands of blue contacts begin to pop up. Soon they would disappear as they activated their slip drives. By doing so, they would destroy any ounce of progress humanity had ever made on those celestial bodies they targeted.

I took a breath, conscious of the fact that it could be one of my last. As I exhaled, I felt how pronounced my heartbeat was, now acutely aware of the individual beads of sweat dribbling down my temples. I blinked and saw the walls of the room turn to black. The area of light around me began to shrink.

I was guided down into a chair that appeared beneath me and it was then that I realised I was no longer in the command room, but somewhere else. Somewhere dark and cold.

I looked to my left and saw that Admiral Krellic sat beside me. General Harland was next to her, with dozens of more people forming a row. I looked down the line of people and saw a mix of officers and ministers. Past them, I recognised the brown uniforms worn by the Mons miliary officers. Director Varlow sitting next to a general of his own whose number of medals put both Harland and Krellic's to shame.

My eyes bolted forwards as the sound of a thundering voice

moved past us. "Forty-two billion lives..." it said in a slow, aggravated tone.

I looked to the centre of this new area we found ourselves in and while I saw nothing, I could feel its presence. The entire universe staring at us. Staring at *me*.

"Forty-two billion lives..." it repeated, this time slower, more ponderous, and with notes of rage, almost as if it was stirring from a slumber.

I saw movement in my peripheral and turned to see Director Varlow stand, his trembling finger pointing to my end of the chamber. "They attacked first; they are to blame and left us no choice."

Part of me was impressed by his bravado; his lack of fear in the face of the entire conceivable universe watching us. But the other part of me—the majority—felt we would be punished for speaking out of turn.

"You are all to blame," the voice spoke again.

My eyes searched the black depths for any sign or shape. A flicker of light or a stirring of dust. But while there was nothing visible, everything was there all at once. Director Varlow was forced down into his seat as the voice washed over him. He grunted with discomfort as his back settled against the hard chairs each of us had materialised into.

"It should not have come to this," the voice said after several agonising seconds. "Now you will watch, and see the fruits you have wrought."

My pulse thundered in my ears and the sense of confusion and misery gave way to hopelessness. The expanse before us brightened in a circular spot no larger than a metre across.

A woman dressed in the vibrant stylings of those worn in the southern provinces of Mars walked to the centre of the light. As she stopped, her red, puffy eyes moved across our faces. Holding back a steady stream of tears she cried, "You did this!"

Flames engulfed her then.

No screams. No pleas for mercy. Only a fire that broke her into ash.

A collective gasp filled the chamber, but no words were uttered, for no one had the strength to speak. Then, as if she had never existed, the circle of light was empty, leaving us in silence.

Another person entered the light. A resident of Europa, judging by the suit he wore. The man looked to each of us before uttering the same words. But while the woman's voice carried sadness, his only conveyed rage as he screamed, "You did this!"

And I felt it. Oh, God, each one of those words was like an ice pick shoved into my mind. I saw him turn to flame and ash, just as the woman had. My fingers curled over the armrests of the chair as the group cried out again.

The sense of loss I felt could not be accurately conveyed by such an artificial construct as words. It was as if a spark had burst into being and then been snuffed out without a trace. Such a waste of something so precious, so fleeting.

As the ash fizzled and popped into nothingness, the next person emerged from the dark. A little girl no older than six ran into the light. Her aura of excitement was accentuated by her pink jacket and fuzz-topped boots.

She turned and looked at us.

"No!" I screamed. "No! No!" I bolted up and bounded towards the light. I grabbed the girl, hugging her in a vain attempt to shield her from what was coming. "No more of this! Please!"

I went to pull the child away from that horrific place, but I felt myself being separated from her as I was dragged backwards towards my chair. I tried to grab her again, but my arms refused to comply.

As my spine made contact with chair, the voice spoke again. "Forty-two billion."

I let out a wail of grief as the little girl looked to us. "You did this!" she proclaimed, before bursting into a funeral pyre.

I screamed and yelled, trying to stand, but could not move as this invisible force kept me pinned where I sat. I realised then that we would be forced to witness the deaths of every single soul our actions impacted.

Despite my cries of protest, and the shrieks of pain from the others in my group, the line of deaths continued.

None were spared—not the old, the young, the weak, the strong. Not even the babes who had breathed their first breath mere minutes prior. But while these children could not talk nor walk, the intense focus in their eyes told us everything we needed to know.

We did this.

As soul after soul was brought to flame, it would be easy to assume we became desensitised to it. Blunt to the grim amount of violence and death. But this could not be farther from the truth, for I felt every single one of them. All forty-two billion. Not even the sensation of hunger or thirst was there to take our collective minds from what was occurring before us. We could only focus on the flame, one by one, coming for them all.

As the last person faded to ash, the light went out and we sat in exhausted grief.

There was a flash, forcing me to slam my eyelids shut until it passed. I opened them slowly, terrified of what lay in store for us next.

I realised I was upright, staring into my bathroom mirror. My eyes gravitated to the small clock projected against the glass. The date was familiar, and I remembered why. It was the morning of the meeting when I had been informed of the missile sites on Luna.

I stood there and watched as droplets of blood slowly leaked from my nose and dripped into the white sink basin. My mind struggled to process the emotions in the unfathomable amount of time that had passed.

I let the feelings wash over me as I wiped my bloody nose with a thick wad of toilet paper. I knew I would attend the meeting General Harland had called for that day. Even if it took everything I had—everything my future self had—I would be attending that meeting.

I knew that under no circumstances would I order any weapons to be fired. I would not have the ashes of billions on my hands. Even if the Mons government fired at us, I would never retaliate. My people may die, and I could not control the actions of others, but the innocents on the other side would live, and I knew that needed to be enough.

They were not the ones responsible for the actions of their government, so why should they bear the brunt of it?

I would never allow that to happen.

---

I went to the meeting in a daze. I passed by secretaries and security officers, each nodding to me as they always did. Some made idle conversation, but I heard nothing and saw even less.

As I sat in the meeting, I could see that my ministers and officers looked entirely like I did: stunned and absent.

Admiral Krellic was not present and General Harland looked as if he had spent the entire morning throwing up. We sat in silence for an hour, two hours, none of us wanting to speak of our shared experience. To put it into words would guarantee we would sever our own threads to sanity and sail off towards the endless horizon of madness.

*Even if we spoke, would we have the words to convey the unperceivable?*

The younger officers looked to each other, wondering why no one was saying anything. A few nervous coughs here, several harsh whispers there. But I hardly noticed them, my mind remaining in that dark chamber.

As the sun left the windows outside, I built up the courage to speak. "General," I said. Harland looked as if he was going to throw up again. "You called this … meeting." I could hardly get the words out, fighting with myself to stop from breaking down.

Harland nodded. "Luna... The missiles..." he replied. I had never heard his voice sound so fragmented before. His voice hardly more than an absent whisper, he looked to the officer in charge of the main screen and said, "Show me the live images of the sites."

As the junior officer complied, the screen filled with the moon's surface. The crackling of the deciphered mirage barriers showed the surface below. My brow furrowed as I could see teams carrying equipment scurrying around the site—the missiles having been already loaded onto trucks that sat nearby.

"They're dismantling them," I said.

"The next site," Harland interjected, his voice containing a spark of life. "Show me another."

The projectionist compiled and switched the view to a different location. It was the same outcome.

The missiles were gone.

General Harland ordered that each site be shown, and each was the same. I stood up after a moment and said, "There is nothing to discuss then."

I moved into the hallway and headed for the bathroom. A single thought tumbling through my mind:

*I need to meet with Director Varlow. I need to look him in the eye and discuss a continued peace. Even if we say nothing, the mutual understanding will be there. Every missile, every bomb, every weapon will need to be dismantled and cast into the dirt.*

I entered the bathroom and sealed the stall. A quivering breath was all it took for the dam to break, and then I wept. I wept for hours, knowing just how close we had come.

# AN EPILOGUE TO THE UNFINISHED

"What the hell does that say?" Murphy asked as he bobbed a cigarette between his lips.

"Can you not smoke in here?" Nevil's reply came as a question, but was intended as a statement. "These are the original drafts; there are no copies."

Murphy rolled his eyes and expelled the smoke though his nose. "I know that, that's why you're here!" he barked. A moment passed before he added, "And when was the last time you heard of a house fire because of some cigarette ash?"

Nevil ignored his boss's previous statement and chose to acknowledge the one prior. "As to what it says…" He trailed off as he picked up the paper and squinted at the words. "Hell, I know I'm the expert on her handwriting, but near the end of her life, her penmanship really went downhill. I think it's called 'A Rose Among Men,' but that word could be *noose*." He pointed at the doctor-like script on the second word of the title. "I'll have to study it more."

Murphy took a step to the right, his hand batting away some unseen dust. "I can't believe the printing house estimates for this project. A bunch of strips of stories, rough drafts, and journal entries all collected into a book, and they expect it to sell millions. They're planning to call it *The Lost Works of Eileen Ellenson.*"

Nevil put down the various papers gently on the scuffed desk. "But it begs the question of whether she would have wanted these to be released at all. She clearly shelved them for a reason. Some of the things we found in the study are from the early sixties."

Murphy shrugged. "If she didn't want them released, why hold on to them for thirty years?" He pointed around the room, his cigarette ash fluttering to the shabby hardwood floor. "She should have burned them, or at the very least, mentioned in her will that she didn't want them released." Then, under his breath Murphy added, "Or had children so they could look after her estate better."

Nevil sent a cat-eyed expression towards the man. "I hardly think we can blame a dying woman for not remembering stories she penned over three decades prior. She probably forgot about them."

"Exactly my point. And now the publishing house will remember them on her behalf."

"I don't know, it just seems a little like grave robbing to me. Not to mention capitalising on name rec—"

"Not just *a* name; *the* biggest name in American literature since Harvey Dowell. But I don't need to tell you," Murphy said, giving Nevil a peculiar glance. "You're her biggest fan."

Nevil tilted his head. "The publishing house would call me her biographer or a critic, but sure, I guess I'm a fan." He gave an exasperated breath that his life's passion could be condensed to something so trivial as simple fandom. "But I must say, I always enjoyed her older stuff—the works she wrote in her thirties. Her shorter works especially."

"Oh, yes, that's all fine and dandy," Murphy said, as he opened various leather-bound journals scattered around the library. "This might as well be in Hebrew. I can't make heads or tails of what any of it says."

Nevil's lips thinned in annoyance before he changed the subject, "The things I was reading in the study really struck a chord with me. The date on it meant it must have been in consideration for *Of Broken Secrets*. If that story had been in there, who knows how much better that already stellar collection would have been. I wonder why she shelved it?"

Murphy shrugged and tossed a binder to the wooden table-top. "You know those artist types, always their biggest critics. But the fans are clamouring for this stuff, and we'll give it to them alright."

Nevil moved over to the binder Murphy had tossed aside. He flipped through page after page of the notes and stories. "From my first impressions alone, I think we might even have enough for two volumes of lost content. And finding those notes and lost chapters to end the *Chaucer Bridge* series is something else entirely. We just need to find a writer that can stitch it all together and tie up the loose ends."

Murphy perked up, pulling the cigarette from his lips. "Jacqueline Carvey worked with her before on um..." He snapped his fingers. "What's the book they wrote together?"

"*The Violet Letter*?" Nevil offered the answer to such an obvious question.

"Yes, yes. That one. Jacqueline would no doubt jump at the chance." He paused, looking at the piles of books and papers scattered around the room. "Three books—not too shabby. Plus, those journal entries." He let out a dry chuckle. "We can't ignore them. The good ones at least, before she lost her damn marbles."

"She did not 'Loose her damn marbles'!" Nevil barked. "She just had some issues. Who doesn't? Losing her husband and then her only sibling within a six-month span affected her deeply."

"Right," Murphy said, holding up his palms in the form of mock surrender. "Fine. She was affected, got it." He shook his head before opening another drawer. He placed the cigarette back between his lips and began to shuffle around several pieces of aged paper. "Well, I'm gonna call Gus with the good news that this little exercise wasn't a complete waste. Three books minimum, probably more," Murphy proclaimed with a grin on his face, turning to head into the hallway.

Nevil looked at the old notebooks he had piled on the corner of the desk. Hundreds of thousands of words, all left unseen by the public.

*Who knows how many hundreds of hours of human life were dedicated to them?* Nevil thought as he patted the tall stack. *She had a reason for keeping them shelved, but the reader in me wants to devour them all. There are some real gems in the bit that I've read so far.*

He looked out the window toward the summer day that radiated down the quiet boulevard outside.

*I guess this just shows how much talent Eileen had. The fact that even her castaways are better than most writers' greatest accomplishments. The fans want them, but the artist didn't want them to be seen. A curious notion.*

He moved over to a bookcase on the far side of the room and grabbed a letter bound journal, dated 1960. He smiled at it.

*The year her first book was published.*

---

Nevil sat in his high-rise office at Newport Publishing. His hands straddled the armrests of his chair as he studied the soft rains that crept in from the Midwest outside. Life was good. His raise had come through last week and he already had big plans for what to do with the boost.

He looked to his watch. It was quarter to five. He had one last document to sign off on before he finished his quota for the day.

The desk phone rang and he turned in his chair and lifted the phone to his ear. "Nevil speaking," he said in a pleasant tone.

"Nevil, come see me please." Murphy's distinctive drawl could be heard flooding though the receiver. "It's urgent."

Nevil contemplated reminding his boss that he was off soon,

but thought better of it. "May I ask what this is about?" he asked instead, his voice sounding tired—almost defeated—knowing he would most likely be staying late again.

"The Ellenson collection, of course. What else could it be?"

*It could have to do with the two novels and three poetry books I'm also involved in at the moment,* he thought as he hung up the receiver with little care. He stood, brushing off a piece of dust that clung to his sport coat. Its presence mildly disturbed him.

He walked down the hall, passing a collection of cubicles, and exchanged pleasantries with a cataloguer before he arrived at Murphy's door. He glanced to the empty secretary desk nearby.

His knuckles had barely made contact with the wood when Murphy bellowed, "You don't need to knock, Nevil; I've told you, come in."

Nevil opened the door gingerly and felt the cold breeze of Murphy's office hit him in the face, sending a chill down his spine. Nevil knew of Murphy's fascination with storms and how he always kept windows open so he could appreciate them fully.

Murphy sat with his back to the door, his eyes watching the storm move thought the high-rises before him, a cigarette burning idle between his index and middle finger. To Nevil, the vice president looked like an emperor marvelling at his lands before him.

"The reviews are in," Murphy said abruptly, spinning around in his chair. His words scurried out the sliver of an open window beside him.

Nevil squinted. "We went over them last week. The pre-release copies, remember?"

"Not the press reviews; the ones from the people. The actual readers—the paying general public. They are unanimous…" He trailed off, drawing a puff from his cigarette. "They love the sequencing, love the stories. I was right to give you that raise." Murphy nodded in self-satisfaction at his own words. "Yes, sir, you really took a bunch of dusty scraps and made it into a show of force. No doubt about it."

"Thank you," Nevil said, leaning over the back of the maroon leather chair that sat across from Murphy's desk. But why is this urgent?" he asked, clearing his throat. "I appreciate the praise, of course, but I don't—"

Murphy pointed at him, a smile tugging at the corners of his mouth. "Because of what you wrote."

"What I wrote? I—"

Murphy clicked his tongue several times. "Don't play the fool, old boy. You're clever and I know the fans are eating it up. I just wish you would have told me that you put that in there."

Nevil searched the room as if the plastic potted plants would offer him some sort of clarification. The curtains rippled from the breeze that brushed against them. "Murphy, I really don't know what you mean."

"What? You're going to say you didn't put it there?" Murphy's face hardened. "Who else could have? You approved the final manuscripts and sent it to the presses. Really now, if you didn't want to get caught, you should have distanced your-self better than that." Murphy held up a hand as Nevil opened his mouth to speak. "But I'm not mad. Really, I'm not. I'm impressed. You sounded just like her."

Nevil chewed his lip as he tried to recall the mental image of giving the final formatted manuscripts the required once over. He could not for the life of him fathom what Murphy was on about.

"I really am at a loss as to what you're referring to," he said after a moment.

Murphy sized up his subordinate before looking him in the eyes. There was a sigh and then, "Fine, if we must do it this way: the 'Note From the Author.'" He bent his fingers in air quotes.

Nevil stayed silent so Murphy continued, "The note at the back discussing the unpublished nature of the stories. The way Eileen—a.k.a. you—talked about the company scrounging and finding the manuscripts. Stories that were forgotten about, discarded. But now thirty years later, she has realised they are publishable after all, and she had given us her blessing." Murphy smirked. "Genius! You gave us some extra credibility, and again I say, you sounded just like her. All the fans are talking about this note, many saying it must be the last thing she wrote before she passed. So again, I say *bravo*."

Nevil swallowed a lump in his throat. "Can I see this note?"

Murphy searched his desk for a quick second before saying, "Well, I don't have a copy. I only read it a few hours ago when Nancy passed on the reviews. She showed me the note in her copy when I asked more about it."

He leaned forward and pressed the intercom button on the phone beside him. He sat in silence for a moment, before quickly releasing the button. "Sorry, I let her go home early. White as a sheet, the poor girl. Some sort of flu, she said." He paused, leaning back in his chair, his eyes narrowing as he added, "But why would you want to—"

"Because I did not write it," Nevil said with a drawn-out cadence.

Murphy blinked several times. "No one else had the final say on that manuscript and no one else could have sounded enough like her to convince all the fans."

"Murphy, I swear, it wasn't me."

Murphy shook his head. "Fine, that's right, I get it. You want to preserve your little fantasy about Eileen Ellenson." He crossed his arms, his head tilting as he added, "Let me guess, she came to you in a vision and told you to write it? Or better yet, her ghost slipped those pages into the manuscript?"

Murphy laughed for a long time before saying, "Go home, Nevil. And while you're there, see if you can dig out your Ouija board and find out if she can write you another note for that novel Jacqueline Carvey is putting together. Better yet, have her write a prequel to *Dawn's Dream*." He laughed again. "You experts are always a funny bunch. I'll be laughing all the way to the bank though!"

Nevil took a long and deliberate breath, keeping his opinions to himself. He turned and left the office, the sounds of Murphy letting out another guffaw of laughter roaring down the hall after him.

But instead of going home as he had been instructed, Nevil headed towards to the basement where the printing presses were. He needed to see this note for himself, and what better place than at the source?

---

Nevil moved about the various presses and spinning reels of paper. He understood not every book produced by the publishing house was printed out of these basement presses, but he did know that the book he sought was here.

He walked up a set of steel stairs and moved across the scaffolding over a set of binding machines. Several workers did a double take, but upon seeing his mint condition white hard hat, looked away with vague disinterest.

He arrived at the plant supervisor's closed door and knocked. The plastic blinds on the opposite side of the window shot up, and Tony's thin face emerged. His eyes showed a range of emotions upon recognising Nevil. First confusion, then annoyance, before finally landing on curiosity.

He opened the door, the smell of cigar smoke wafting after him.

"Mr. Chapman," he said in his usual accented tone. He looked at his watch. "Shouldn't you office workers be packing up for the day?" Before Nevil could get a word in, Tony continued, "Don't tell me Murphy granted you an overtime incentive; that would be a lie." He chuckled, stepping out of the doorway and allowing Nevil to enter.

Nevil took a confident step into the shabby office and shook his head. "No, I've come here of my own accord." He waited for Tony to close the door before adding, "It's about Seventeen dash, um, two four."

Tony frowned as he moved behind his desk and grabbed the half-chewed, half-smoked cigar from the ashtray on his desk. "I need English. Down here we don't speak in code."

Without waiting for the last syllable to leave Tony's mouth, Nevil replied, "Eileen Ellenson's Anthology."

"Well, what about it?" Tony asked, the cigar bobbing at the corner of his mouth. "We're right on schedule." He looked through the glass wall to this left, the plant humming away below. "Even with printer sixteen down." He paused, his eyes returning to Nevil's clean-shaven face. "Say, when are the replacement parts coming from Detroit? I've had a work order in for weeks and—"

Nevil held up his hand. "Call Chris or Mike. I'm not here to talk about that." He lowered his hand and looked over his shoulder. "Who else has access to the manuscript master plates?"

Tony pulled the cigar from his lips and put it back in the ashtray. "Well, me, of course. But Dillion is our lead operator. I assigned him to set up the blanks and reels for this project.

"So Dillion is the guy I need to talk to. He's here today, right?"

Tony nodded, prompting Nevil to pivot. As his hand made contact with the brass handle, Tony's voice came from behind, "You mind telling me what this is about?"

Nevil felt his grip loosen on the knob. "A page has been added to the manuscript during printing. Multiple readers have reported it. I-I want to see it and fix it. Remove it, I guess would be a more accurate term."

"Well if you need to see the plates the printers are using, let's just head down and have a look, shall we?"

"I would much rather talk to Dillion first."

Tony stood, running a hand though his salt-and-pepper coloured hair as he said, "Let's see what we are dealing with before we hunt down my best employee and start accusing him of something."

"Very well," Nevil said through a sigh. "Lead the way."

The two men exited the office and moved across the scaffolding before descending a set of stairs that led to the eastern corner of the basement. Nevil heard the internals of the machines around him rumbling as they diligently worked. Paper whipped by as it moved from one rack to another.

"Here we are," Tony said, gesturing to the mammoth-sized printers, having to yell in order to be heard. "The plates are obviously in them now, but the duplicate sets are in this office here. That's what you want to see, right?"

"These are the same as the ones in the machines?" Nevil asked, his eyes moving from the conveyors overhead to a worn-looking door.

Tony nodded, his hands already on the handle. "Yup, exactly the same."

Nevil watched as Tony pushed the door open and both men entered the room. Apart from a desk in the middle, every inch of wall space was occupied by large filing cabinets. Tony closed the door behind them to block out the noise from the printers outside.

Nevil scanned the faces of the cabinets. "These aren't all for—"

"No, of course not," Tony interrupted. "We've got eight other books on the go and several that we just ceased the print run for." He pointed to the filing cabinets along the right-hand wall. "The ones in there are going to the storage depot next week." He gestured with his chin to a set of cabinets on the opposite side of the room. "Ellenson's stuff is in there. They're labelled, so…" He trailed off as Nevil took several deliberate paces forward and began opening drawers.

Nevil moved the metal plates from one side of the cabinet to the other as his eyes scanned the etchings. As he reached the final set of plates, his eyes darted around the open drawer.

"It's not here," he said as his eyes scanned the closing words on the final story. "There must be more plates, or one missing, or—"

"Which one you got in your hand there?" Tony asked, taking a step forward.

"Three hundred thirty-three," Nevil replied, his eyes searching the cabinet for an additional plate.

"Well, that's the last one. Easy to remember, lots of threes in that number."

Nevil licked his lips in frustration. Taking a step back, he said, "I need to see the complete and bound books."

As he moved towards the exit, Tony held out his hand, blocking the door. "Look, I've humoured you, I've let you see the copies. What's going on?"

"I told you; an additional page has—"

"Ya, 'been added' and people are reporting it. Is this page vulgar or something? Typos galore? Why all the—"

"Fine! Fine…" Nevil started. He crossed his arms across his chest. "There's an author's note at the back of the book that wasn't there when I approved the manuscript for print. I want to know where it came from, and more importantly, who wrote it."

Tony screwed up his face. "And you're sure you checked that original file? Quality control is a big issue to us down here. I can speak for all of my staff: If there's a page in the book, it's because it was part of the manuscript your people handed us."

Nevil chewed his lip before replying, "I went through that book backwards and forwards. I could quote most of it. this author's note was not present when I approved it."

Tony stepped away from the door, his face stern. Nevil seized the handle and pulled it open. The two men moved outside the storage room and headed to the right. Tony walked with a quickened pace that Nevil struggled to keep up with.

They moved onto the loading dock and Tony pointed a finger towards several stacks of boxes that had yet to be loaded onto pallets. The supervisor mumbled a word to himself, before walking forward. He pulled a small knife from his belt and cut the tape of the top box that sat at chest level.

"These ones are going to Chastain's tonight. Let's have a look." He pulled the first book from the box and flipped to the back. his eyes narrowed for a brief moment before passing it to Nevil. "Well, that was a waste of time," he said under his breath.

Nevil looked at the book in his hands. At the back were two blank pages. No sign of any author's note, just cream-coloured paper gazing up at him. Nevil closed the book. "We must have spooked him; he must know that we're onto him."

"These were printed hours ago," Tony said. "There is no way that whoever is behind this sort of thing would be able to—"

Nevil pulled on the two blank pages, his eyes moving up to meet Tony's. "Why are these extra pages here?"

"Part of the process. Every paper has a twin, so the front matter stuff, table of contents, legal page, those all have twin pages at the back of the book. Just the way it is in the making and assembly process. I guess there's not enough content to fill those sister pages."

"Can we get rid of them?"

Tony's face shifted to an unamused look before saying, "Not unless you want the entire book reformatted. Not to mention remaking all the plates and starting all the process over again. That's a lot of work and money for two measly blank pages to be removed." Nevil went to speak but Tony persisted. "I guarantee you, look at your bookshelf when you get home. Five out of ten will have at least one extra page in it. Like I said, it's part of the manufacturing process."

Nevil lowered the book. "You mind if I keep this?"

Tony shrugged. "I'll replace it and mark it down in the records that it was below acceptable quality."

Nevil nodded in thanks. "I'm going to get to the bottom of this. You let me know if you come across anything."

Tony began to follow him out of the loading dock and onto the printing floor. "I'm not going to lie, you've caught my attention by just how far you're chasing this thing," he said before the sounds of the presses swallowed his words up.

---

Nevil's keys jangled as he inserted one of them into his front door's lock. The entire ride home, he had thought of heading to the local bookstore and scouring their copies of the Eileen's posthumous anthology, but he kept coming to the same conclusion. *If the author's note is there, then that doesn't prove anything I didn't already know. And if it's not there then it's just from a new batch.*

He entered his house and walked down the hall to the kitchen. He plopped the Ellenson book Tony had given him onto the counter and opened his alcohol cabinet. One sealed bottle of whisky he had received as a part of a secret Santa gift two years prior looked down at him from its perch.

"I don't need a drink; I need answers," he said aloud as he shut the cabinet.

Nevil moved about the living room, tidying up an already spotless room in an attempt to take his mind from the conundrum. All these remedial tasks did was allow the idea to fester.

"They must have altered the plates," he mumbled to himself as he alphabetised his small collection of VHS tapes. "There is no other feasible way. Another plate was made and then removed after the first few batches." Nevil knew the chances of that were low, but it was the only idea that stuck. "Someone would notice. Tony would have to have been involved somehow. But who would go to all this work? And what would be the motive?"

Nevil abandoned his make-work task and began to prepare himself a small dinner.

"But I have a good sense of people. I don't think Tony was lying. Besides, he's hardly an Ellison fan if I remember correctly from the time he talked books with me last year. So again, what would be the motive? There is none."

Nevil realised he had been on automatic for at least an hour.

ROBERT J. BRADSHAW

In that time, he had eaten, cleaned the dishes, and was in the process of brushing his teeth. He looked at himself in the mirror. "Tomorrow, I'll figure it out. I won't think about it anymore tonight."

As he lay in bed, he attempted to rid his mind of this latest fixation. He was unsuccessful.

Nevil was stirred awake in the way only a full bladder can manage. He slowly raised his arms and pushed the blanket from himself, his right eye opening and seeing that it was still dark out. A brief flash of excitement came over him at the prospect of having several hours of sleep still ahead of him. He stood, moving to the door of his bedroom in a slow stagger. Opening it, he moved past the short hall that looked into the kitchen.

His eyes registered the book before his legs did. He took two more steps before stopping abruptly. He was wide awake now.

Nevil stepped back, his eyes locked onto the counter where the hardcover was splayed open. Two lit candles kept the book from closing. He gulped and inched forward.

*Did I do that? When I was lost in thought did I—*

He stopped dead in his tracks. The back page was displayed. One that previously sat empty but was now full of words. Clearly labelled at the top: "A Note From The Author."

"Jesus!" he said in a muffled cry. He reached out and removed the candles, which prompted the cover to snap shut. Picking up the book, he turned to the back pages, his eyes skimming in stunned disbelief over the words. "How—" he begun to say as the sound of his voice moved about the silent kitchen.

As he finished the last line that thanked New Era Publishing for releasing the stories, his eyes snapped up.

*Someone swapped out the books,* he thought, letting the anthology fall though his fingers, landing hard on the counter. *Someone is in my house.*

He turned and ran to the front door. It was sealed and the deadbolt was still in place. He looked over his shoulder to ensure no one was behind him. His pulse throbbed in his neck as

96

he moved back towards the kitchen. He threw on every light switch within reach, before moving into the living room. It was empty, save for the piles of VHS tapes still in their unfinished alphabetised state that stared back at him.

Nevil took a sharp left and hurried down the hall to his study. He pushed open the door and snapped on the light. No one was there either.

His pulse began to level out, but as he turned to leave, his eyes lingered on the desk. A sheet of paper sat squarely between two binders of manuscripts. Nevil knew these binders had not been placed at random, for they contained the pages discovered inside Eileen Ellenson's estate.

*I put those away,* he thought as he checked the corners of the room. *I know I did.*

He moved forward, his eyes trained on the single sheet of white paper and the handwritten words upon it. He rounded his desk so could make out the cursive more clearly. There was no doubt in his mind to whom it belonged. It was written in the clear, swooping stylings of Eileen as she had done so in the sixties and seventies before her health declined so drastically.

Trembling, he leaned over his desk, placing a shaking arm out for support. His eyes went over each word with surgical precision.

DEAR NEVIL,

I MUST SAY THIS IS QUITE A FIRST FOR ME, WRITING A LETTER AFTER I HAVE PASSED. WHILE I HAVE MET MANY A DEVOTED FAN IN MY TIME, I'VE NEVER BEEN INSIDE ONE OF THEIR HOMES. AFTER ADDING MY NOTE TO YOUR COPY OF MY "NEW" ANTHOLOGY, I TOOK A LOOK AT YOUR BOOKSHELVES. I WAS MOST IMPRESSED THAT YOU OWNED A COPY OF ALL MY WORKS, ALL OF WHICH ARE FIRST EDITIONS, AND I COULD TELL THEY'VE BEEN READ SEVERAL TIMES.

BUT THIS IS, OF COURSE, NOT WHY I AM WRITING THIS LETTER…

I WANTED TO CONGRATULATE YOU ON THE ANTHOLOGY. I DID NOT LIE WHEN I SAID I HAD INDEED FORGOTTEN ABOUT MANY OF THOSE STORIES, NOR DID I FIB WHEN I MENTIONED HOW IMPRESSED I WAS

WITH HOW THEY HELD UP. I APPRECIATE YOUR HARD WORK AND YOUR DEDICATION IN BRINGING MY STORIES BACK FROM THE GRAVE, OR IS THAT PHRASE INAPPROPRIATE GIVEN MY CURRENT STANDING?

BUT NEVIL, THERE IS ANOTHER REASON FOR WRITING THIS LETTER. I WANT TO TALK ABOUT THE SECOND COLLECTION YOU HAVE PLANNED. THERE ARE THREE STORIES IN THERE THAT I DID NOT FORGET ABOUT. IN FACT, I VERY MUCH REMEMBER THEM.

I HATE THEM.

I WROTE THEM AS A CHANGE OF STYLE, OR PRACTICE, OR AS AN EXPERIMENT. THE REASON WHY IS NOT IMPORTANT, AS I'VE LONG FORGOTTEN THE ORIGINAL INTENTION. BUT I NEED YOU TO KNOW THAT I WROTE THEM IN A MISALIGNED HEADSPACE. I REGRET NOT DISCARDING THEM YEARS AGO BUT I HAD A POLICY TO NEVER DESTROY ANY OF MY WORKS AFTER I BURNED ALL THOSE DALTON CLIFFORD STORIES. OH, HOW I REGRETTED THAT BLUNDER FOR YEARS AFTER!

NEVIL, THIS IS VERY IMPORTANT. THE STORIES "A DARKNESS AT MIDDAY," "THE SUMMERFORD TALE," AND "COME TIDINGS AND CHEER" ARE NOT TO SEE THE LIGHT OF DAY. I CANNOT STRESS THIS ENOUGH.

TO PUT IT SIMPLY, THEY ARE NOT ME. IF THEY ARE RELEASED, THEY WILL BE RANKED AGAINST THE TOTALITY OF MY WORK AND I JUST CANNOT BEAR TO SEE IT. THEY WILL BE HATED, PLACED AT THE BOTTOM OF LISTS AND RIGHTFULLY SO. MY DEVOTED FANS WILL NO DOUBT THINK LESS OF ME AFTER READING THEM. I WOULD RATHER MY REPUTATION STAY MORE INTACT THAN RELEASE THAT GARBAGE.

WITH THOSE REMOVED, THIS NEXT COLLECTION YOU HAVE PLANNED SITS AT THIRTEEN STORIES. YOU CAN RAISE THAT NUMBER BY ONE WHEN YOU ADD ANOTHER STORY. ONE YOU LEFT UNFOUND IN MY HOUSE, TITLED, "HEARTFELT HOPES."

IT IS MIXED IN WITH SEVERAL TAX DOCUMENTS IN A BOX IN THE ATTIC. I HAD DISCOVERED THE STORY A FEW SUMMERS AGO AND MEANT TO PUT IT IN WITH SOME OF MY FOLDERS BUT MY MIND WAS NOT AT ITS BEST THOSE LAST FEW YEARS.

WHEN YOU FIND THE STORY, I WILL WRITE TO YOU AGAIN. TAKE CARE, ITS ALWAYS NICE TO CONVERSE WITH A FAN.

*WITH LOVE,*

*— EILEEN ELLENSON*

As Nevil finished reading the letter, he felt like he was going to faint. He blinked several times, struggling to believe this was real and not part of some elaborate dream. He lifted his head and looked to the open door and the dark hallway beyond. He gulped.

*Is she still there?* he wondered, listening to the sounds of the night.

He looked down at the binder on the right. It was the one that contained the stories Eileen had specifically mentioned in her letter.

*They weren't bad,* Nevil thought. *Not at all. I really enjoyed "Come Tidings and Cheer."*

He flipped though the plastic covered originals, his eyes stopping for a moment as he reached the first tale that had been on the receiving end of Eileen's scorn: "A Darkness At Midday." He remembered how at first it seemed as if the subject matter was unlike anything Eileen had ever written before. But Murphy had been clear; any story discovered was going to be collected. Even those that were noticeably unfinished would be put into some anthology at some point.

Nevil reflected on how it, despite being rough around the edges, was a fascinating snapshot into Eileen's mindset at a time when she was still a lowly writer and not the legend she would soon become.

Nevil left the study and moved towards his bedroom, still conscious that Eileen's spectre could be lurking around any corner.

He stopped in front of the bedroom door, his mind racing. *Well, I can't sleep now,* he thought, as he entered the room and changed quickly. In a flash he moved to the front door, grabbing only his jacket and keys. He needed to lay eyes on the story that Eileen had said he had missed in the attic.

---

The key was in the lockbox, just as it had been the day of the funeral. Due to Eileen having no living relatives, the house sat in limbo. The bank and the city had argued back and forth as to if it should be turned into a historic location, a tourist attraction, or simply be bought and sold like any building of brick and plaster.

Nevil let himself in the vacant house and quickly switched on the lights. *Someone has been paying the power bill,* he thought as he observed the light fixture above him with a curious glance.

The entire car ride from his house, Nevil had been mentally preparing for his journey to the attic. As much as he was afraid of Eileen's spirit, the fear was outweighed by the intrigue of the unknown. So far, she had shown no sign of hostility or violence towards him, and with that knowledge as his shield, he took the flight of stairs up to the second level with confidence.

The attic entrance was a pulldown trapdoor on the ceiling. As Nevil pulled the cord, a ladder unfolded, landing at his feet. He could hardly imagine an elderly Eileen scaling the rickety structure in her failing health, but then again, Eileen had been full of surprises her entire life.

Nevil climbed the ladder and crawled up into the attic. He pulled on the drawstring overhead, prompting the dirty bulb to illuminate the cramped space. Directly in the centre of the attic was a stained carboard box labeled, "Tax forms."

Nevil tilted his head in surprise. That box had not been so clearly visible when he had stuck his head up on the day of the funeral. A thick layer of dust clung to every container scattered around the space, except for the box in question. No doubt Eileen was helping him.

He ventured forward and removed the lid. As further proof

of her assistance from beyond the grave, a typed and stapled manuscript was sitting on top of a pile of papers.

He pulled the manuscript from the box. As he did so, a folded piece of parchment slid to the floor. The colour of the folded paper was newer and less worn and handled than the manuscript he held in his hands. Any doubt of its origins disappeared as he unfolded the note and recognised the handwriting immediately.

HELLO NEVIL,

I'M GLAD YOU FOUND IT, BUT I MUST SAY I AM DISAPPOINTED YOU DID NOT REMOVE THE THREE STORIES FROM THE BINDER LIKE I ASKED YOU TO. I WANT TO SEE THEM TURNED TO ASH. THAT IS MY REQUEST SO MY FANS CAN NEVER READ THEM.

I HOPE YOU ENJOY "HEARTFELT HOPES." THERE IS A LOT OF YOUTHFUL NOSTALGIA IN THERE. A LOT OF MEMORIES CAME BACK TO ME WHEN I WROTE IT ALL THOSE YEARS AGO. IT IS CERTAINLY BETTER THAN "COME TIDINGS AND CHEER." I EXPECT THIS WILL BE THE LAST TIME YOU HEAR FROM ME AS ONCE THESE STORIES ARE GONE I HAVE NO REASON TO BOTHER YOU ANY LONGER.

GOOD LUCK, NEVIL. I HOPE THE FUTURE STAYS BRIGHT FOR YOU.

— EILEEN

Nevil looked around the attic as a nervous sweat started to pool on his back. *I need to say something,* he thought, his hands trembling. *I need to tell her how wrong she is.*

He stood there for a moment, building up the nerve to speak before he eventually said, "Eileen, if you can hear me..." He paused. The words echoed around the drab attic and while Nevil waited for a response, he could hear a slight breeze knocking against the north facing wall. "You're wrong about 'Come Tidings and Cheer.' Wrong about all of those stories. Your fans would love them. I even would go as far as to say 'Come Tidings And Cheer' would be the centre piece of your next collection. One that fans will talk about for years and—"

Something hit Nevil in the head from above. It wasn't heavy, but the suddenness of it surprised him. He looked down as he heard whatever the object had been hit the floor with a dull click. It was another piece of folded paper.

He looked to the rafters above, and while they sat dark and empty, he could sense her presence all around. Nevil felt his pulse thundering in his ears as he unfolded the new note. The ink looked fresh.

*NEVIL, THAT IS KIND OF YOU TO SAY, BUT MY MIND IS MADE UP. DESTROY THOSE THREE STORIES OR ELSE YOU CAN'T HAVE THIS ONE. PLEASE DON'T TEST ME.*

Nevil shook his head. "Eileen, you have always been so critical of your own work. I'm sure you've seen the articles calling you a perfectionist." His eyes darted to every corner of the attic, hoping they would stay empty. "Think about the stories in the collection we just released. You shelved them, forgot about them entirely, and people are saying they are up there with the best of your work. Give these stories a chance. They have soul. They deserve to exist. I won't destroy them."

Nevil felt a shift in the air around him, as if the entire atmosphere had changed and not for the better. The manuscript beside him sprung up into the air and shoved itself into the tax box. The lid glided up from the floor and slammed down to cover the box. He gasped as the container was pulled across the attic to a far corner. The noise of cardboard sliding against wood sounded like a hissing snake. The note leapt from his hands and moved off to the same dark corner as the box.

Nevil thought about running from the house, but a mix of curiosity and crippling fear kept him locked in place. Several moments passed before a ball of paper came hurling out of the darkness, bouncing off his forehead.

He lowered a shaking hand and unravelled the note. Eileen had written something new on the reverse side.

*I'VE MADE UP MY MIND, NEVIL. I KNOW WHAT WILL HAPPEN. I JUST KNOW IT! NOW LEAVE AND DON'T COME BACK HERE UNTIL ALL THREE*

*OF THEM ARE NOTHING BUT EMBERS. I APPRECIATE THE LOVELY WORDS, TRULY I DO, BUT I KNOW WHAT I WANT AND I WANT THEM GONE.*

Nevil stood. Clutching the note, he said, "Eileen, I'm going down to your study. I want to talk with you more and … well, I see that we've run out of paper. Give me a sign that you'll meet me down there—"

As he turned, he felt an aggressive breeze blow by his ear.

"I'll take that as a yes," he said as he folded the note and moved to exit the attic.

*She always appreciated good conversation, or so I've heard,* he thought as he began to descend the ladder. *And she knows I'll continue to flatter her stories. Even if she hates them, I've never met a writer who didn't enjoy flattery.*

With a thundering pulse and soaked palms, he arrived at Eileen's study. Nevil recalled that the bulk of his and Murphy's findings on the day of the funeral had originated from this room.

Eileen's red cushioned chair pivoted slightly as he entered, and he knew that Ellen was now occupying the chair across from him. A thick stack of lined paper and a pen lay on the desk between them.

"Hello, Eileen," he said, a quiver in his voice. He took a seat on a chair, noting that the last time he had been in this room, it was littered with papers. Its previous contents lay on the floor beside the desk. He returned his gaze forward to the invisible entity across from him. "I think it is fair to say that you were too hasty to condemn the stories for the first collection."

He paused, expecting the pen to meet paper in a frivolous scratching of swooping letters. But the pen nor the paper moved.

"As I said before," he began cautiously, "I have enjoyed all three of the stories in question. While, yes, 'A Darkness At Midday' is unlike anything else you've ever written, that alone makes it worth saving. Your scholars—the people who have been dissecting and analysing your work for decades—would absolutely eat it up."

Nevil's eyes gravitated to the stack of paper as letters began

103

to appear on the topmost page. He could see in his peripherals that the pen still lay on the desk. The paper then slid from the stack and stopped under Nevil's fingers. The note was simple:

THEY WOULD MOCK ME.

"No, they wouldn't. I've met many of them. They think everything you've written has been a masterpiece, and this would be no exception—"

Words began to appear on the next page of the stack before it too was jettisoned across the table and bounced off his fingertips.

I APPRECIATE YOUR CONFIDENCE IN THEM, BUT TO USE YOUR POINT, WHY TARNISH MY SO-CALLED "PERFECT RECORD"? LEAVE IT AS IT IS; LESS CHANCE SOMEONE WILL HATE IT AND RUIN MY REPUTATION.

Nevil screwed up his face as he looked at the words. "The old Eileen Ellenson would have scoffed if she had heard you say that. Where is the Eileen that in sixty-eight said, 'I view each release as a chance to make new fans. That is my motivation; that is my muse'? Where is she? Because I would like to talk with that version of Eileen."

Nevil watched as the next paper on the pile moved slightly, but no words appeared on it. It was almost as if Eileen had touched it but re-evaluated her decision. The study stayed silent for a long time as Nevil continued to watch the paper to no avail, as it stayed empty.

He couldn't take the silence any longer and said, "Let these stories breathe, Eileen. Trust me, as both a fan and a small-time writer myself, you are being too hard on yourself. These stories are gold; they really are." He paused, clearing his throat before adding, "Even if just one person finds them special, doesn't that make them worth saving?"

The stack of papers stayed still. Nevil's eyes wandered the study, uncertain of what Eileen would do next. His nerves were getting the better of him. He worried that he had said the wrong thing.

There was a creak above him from the attic that caused his

eyes to shoot to the ceiling, but he assumed it to be the wind and returned his gaze to the chair across from him.

"Eileen?" he asked finally.

A manuscript plopped down on the table in front of him with a thud, prompting Nevil to nearly jump out of his skin. His eyes flashed over the title that read, "Heartfelt Hopes." He looked to the chair across from him, the paper atop the stack already filling with words.

*WHEN I ATTENDED MY FUNERAL, I OVERHEARD YOU AND THE MAN YOU WERE WITH TALKING. YOU PIQUED MY INTEREST AND I FOLLOWED YOU BACK HERE. I WAS WORRIED ABOUT SEVERAL STORIES THAT YOU SELECTED FOR THE FIRST ANTHOLOGY BUT I STAYED QUIET AND I'M GLAD I DID, BECAUSE YOU WERE RIGHT. THE RAVING REVIEWS PROVE THAT, AND I FEEL MY AUTHOR'S NOTE COVERED THAT SUCCINCTLY.*

Nevil looked up from the page, despite there being many more words written across it. "How did you do that, anyway? Words on paper with a pen is one thing, but adding typed notes to a book after it has been released and printed is—"

The pen rose from the desk and tapped the paper in front of Nevil in an annoyed "keep reading" fashion.

Nevil gulped before continuing to study the letter.

*I WAS WORRIED ABOUT WHAT WOULD BE THE FINAL BOOK IN THE CHAUCER BRIDGE SERIES. I WAS CONCERNED MY NOTES WOULD BE TOO INCOMPLETE AND MY IDEAS TOO PEDESTRIAN. I FEARED THAT WHOEVER READ IT WOULD THINK, OH, EILEEN. SHE'S LOST IT. AGE REALLY CAUGHT UP TO HER. BUT THEN YOU TURNED OVER WHAT I HAD TO JAQUELINE CARVEY. I WATCHED HER AS SHE READ THOSE HUNDRED AND THIRTY PAGES IN A SINGLE DAY, NOT GOING TO BED UNTIL LATE IN THE MORNING.*

*WHEN SHE WOKE UP THE NEXT DAY, THE FIRST THING SHE DID WAS MAKE A POT OF COFFEE BEFORE POURING OVER MY NOTES. SHE JUMPED TO HER WORD PROCESSOR AND TYPED THE NEXT THREE CHAPTERS IN A MATTER OF HOURS. SHE HAD A PERFECT UNDERSTANDING OF THE CHARACTERS, THE SETTINGS, THE THEMES. I WAS PROUD OF HER, AND HOW MUCH SHE REMEMBERED FROM WHEN WE HAD WORKED TOGETHER*

PRIOR. WHILE SHE'S DEVIATED FROM SOME OF MY IDEAS (IT'S INEVITABLE AS SHE'S NOT PSYCHIC AND I DON'T WANT TO GIVE THE POOR GIRL A HEART ATTACK BY WRITING TO HER AS WELL), IT IS OKAY BECAUSE I LIKE HER IDEAS BETTER THAN MY OWN.

WHAT I'M TRYING TO SAY IN MY LONG-WINDED WAY IS THAT I WAS NERVOUS, BUT SHE TOO PROVED ME WRONG AS WELL.

I TRUST YOU, NEVIL. YOU SAY THESE STORIES ARE GOOD, THAT THEY REALLY HAVE A SOUL AND ARE WORTH EXISTING, THEN FINE, PUT THEM OUT INTO THE WORLD. I RESCIND MY CLAUSE OF HOLDING BACK "HEARTFELT HOPES" UNLESS YOU DESTROYED THE OTHERS. TAKE IT AND PUT IT IN THE SECOND COLLECTION TO MAKE IT FIFTEEN STORIES. I HAVE FAITH IN YOUR OPINION.

Nevil chewed his lip for a moment. "Thank you, Eileen. I know that took a lot." He looked to the manuscript on the desk, the typed title staring back at him. "Will you be around to check the ratings for this second anthology?"

The response was almost instantaneous as a paper flew from the stack.

NO, SADLY I WON'T. MY TIME IS LIMITED. I MADE AN AGREEMENT AND ONCE THIS LAST PROBLEM IS SOLVED, I WILL MOVE ON. I HAVE SEEN WHERE I'M GOING AND I WILL BE HAPPY THERE. I WANTED TO PROTECT MY LEGACY BEFORE I COMMITTED TO LEAVING, BUT I SEE NOW THAT IT WAS ALWAYS IN GOOD HANDS. THANK YOU FOR EVERYTHING, NEVIL. IT WAS A PLEASURE TALKING TO YOU.

YOUR FRIEND,

— EILEEN ELLENSON

Nevil felt the atmosphere of the room shift as the chair stirred slightly. He placed the note on the table and looked out to the dark street beyond the window. He knew he was alone now in that big, empty house.

Nevil nodded at Murphy's secretary as he passed by her desk. "Is he available?" he asked with a soft smile, despite the exhaustion that tugged at his eyes.

"He has nothing scheduled," she replied as her gaze gravitated to the binder held under Nevil's arm.

"Thank you," Nevil said before proceeding to knock on the door, entering only when Murphy replied with a brisk response.

"Hardly nine a.m. and already Nevil is paying me a visit?" Murphy said with a surprising amount of cheer in his voice.

"Yes. I have the working version of the second anthology of Eileen Ellenson's posthumous works," Nevil said as he approached the desk.

Murphy gestured to the chair across from him, a look of surprise on his face. "I'll take it, of course, but the deadline is next week." His eyes moved the calendar on the wall beside him to confirm the date.

"It is next week, yes, but I have it compiled now. Fifteen stories."

"Last time we talked it was fourteen stories." He picked up his mug of coffee and swirled it about, leaning back in his chair. "And you said several of them were quite rough, needing a fair bit of fixing up before it was in any shape for the editors. I expected that number to go down, not up."

Nevil placed the binder on the desk, patting it softly. "I guess they didn't need as much work as I originally thought."

Murphy tilted his head as he licked his teeth. "So where did this lucky fifteenth story come from?"

Nevil stayed silent for a moment until Murphy's gaze became too much to handle. "I found it in Eileen's attic, I—"

Murphy shook his head and sat forward, placing his mug on the desk. "We looked up there; you said there was nothing. Why are you lying to me right now?" His tone was surprisingly soft, despite the word choice.

"I'm not lying. There wasn't anything when we looked, but I

went back and—" Nevil closed his eyes as he knew he shouldn't have let that part slip.

"You went back? Look, I know she was your favorite wordsmith, and it must be hard for you that she died, but that's just odd."

Nevil opened the binder, his voice firm as he thumbed through the plastic-covered pages. "I had a dream that we missed something. I needed to know. The idea of a truly 'lost' Ellenson original haunted me, so to speak. I was right, because I found one."

Murphy's face appeared almost playful. "Oh ya? Show me then."

Nevil, who had anticipated this, removed the manuscript of "Heartfelt Hopes" and handed the papers to Murphy, who eyed the cover page with skepticism. "Paper's off," he said as he turned the page and began reading.

"Pardon?" Nevil replied.

"Different colour. Not as worn as the other ones we saw," Murphy replied, his eyes narrowing.

"I think she wrote this one in the late seventies or early eighties maybe. Most of the ones we found were from much earlier, some were her juvenilia which was stored—"

"You know, for an Ellenson scholar you really don't have her cadence down," Murphy said, flipping several pages ahead.

Nevil readjusted himself in his chair. "I don't follow."

Murphy chuckled. "Oh, come now, she would never have said that." He flicked a finger against a sentence on the page. Murphy lowered the papers to the desk and let out a humour-filled sigh. "You got cocky, Nevil. You did such a good job with that author's note, you thought you could master her style long enough to pen a whole story. But as you are always so quick to point out, she's hard to duplicate." He slid the manuscript over to Nevil and laughed. "Good try, but it needs more time in the oven. I have to say, you've got balls. Trying to pass off your own work as hers." He laughed again. "So, I'll tell the editors that fourteen stories are coming their way?"

Nevil opened and closed his mouth several times, unsure of how to proceed. He chose a calm approach, and eventually said, "It's not mine; she wrote it. It was in the attic, like I said—"

"Sure, it was." Murphy gestured for Nevil to stand. "Cut your losses. It's a good try, really convincing, but you can't fool me. They didn't make me vice president for nothing." He smirked before pointing to the binder and adding, "Now leave this with me and I'll get the editors on it right away. As for this," he lifted the manuscript and handed it to Nevil, "this is your intellectual property," he said with a wink. "Put it in one of your own collections and when you are ready to publish it through New Era Publishing, I'll read it in full then."

Nevil looked at the manuscript in his hands and said simply, "Alright," before moving from the office and out into the hallway, mind racing.

*What would Eileen want me to do with this? She was so proud of it. But I can't fit it in somewhere else like the upcoming poetry and journal book; Murphy will remember. He wouldn't see it as a harmless prank then, but probably as insubordination. That could be a fireable offence.* Nevil rubbed his tired face before nodding politely at an accountant who passed by. *I can't put it in my own book. It's not mine—it would be thievery, plain and simple. But on the other hand, the story would live on. Isn't that the important part? The story itself, not the name on the cover?*

He shook his head, recognising the difference between cloud-gazing philosophy and the reality of the world he lived in.

Nevil entered his office and sat behind his desk, letting out a long sigh as his eyes met the title page of the manuscript. *Why it was never released in its time, I'll never understand. She always thought she was an imposter.* Nevil chuckled to himself as his mind lingered on the thought. *The greatest author of the last fifty years and she felt like she was an imposter.*

He ran a hand though his hair as he whispered to himself, "What am I going to do with this? Stick it in a museum?"

Nevil looked up as there was a knock on the door. The man who pushed the building mail cart stood in the doorway. "Letter for you, Mr. Chapman," he said, leaving the envelope on the desk before resuming his duties of pushing the squeaking cart down the hall.

The envelope contained no return address, only his name in swooping cursive on the front. Nevil ripped open the letter and read every word with a smile on his face.

NEVIL, I HEARD EVERYTHING. I WANT YOU TO KEEP THE MANUSCRIPT AND RELEASE IT WHEN IT'S TIME. I HAVE FAITH THAT YOU'LL KNOW WHEN THAT IS. ALL I ASK IS THAT MY NAME IS ON IT WHEN IT DOES FIND ITS WAY INTO THE WORLD.

BUT, NEVIL, I WANTED TO THANK YOU FOR BELIEVING IN MY WORK, EVEN WHEN I DIDN'T.

WITH LOVE,

— EILEEN

Nevil closed the letter and returned it to the envelope, the grin still clutched to his lips. He looked around the room and said quietly, "Thank you, Eileen." He wasn't sure if she was present, but he hoped all the same.

He looked at the manuscript for several moments, knowing that for the next few years it would once again be confined to darkness. As he studied the name on the title page, he felt a new feeling rise in him. He would be the only person on Earth to personally own a finished Eileen Ellenson original that hadn't been seen by the public. Such a notion was both an honour and something he feared, hoping he could keep it safe until the time was right. Whenever that would be.

———

Eleven months to the day, Eileen Ellenson's second posthumous anthology was released, entitled *Whispers From Friends Past*. It soared to the top of the book charts. Several reviews called it better than the first, with many citing "Come Tidings and Cheer" as an "Instant Ellenson Classic."

Many other publications listed "A Darkness at Midday" as the number one, must-read story of the year. A prominent writer went on record saying, "Ellenson has never before attempted a tale invoking such an innovative tone ... absolutely dripping in atmosphere."

"The Summerford Tale" was also well received, with many people speculating that it was the middle piece in a previously unseen trilogy of tales, revolving around an unnamed girl venturing through the English countryside. One publication claimed that, "'The Summerford Tale' will put the few naysayers that claim Ellenson wasn't simply the best to rest."

As for "Heartfelt Hopes," Nevil did release it when the time came. As soon as Murphy retired, Nevil ensured the story found its way into Eileen Ellenson's fifth and final posthumous release as an epilogue of sorts. But even with the story gone from his possession, he was happy that Eileen's last tale finally managed to join its siblings out in the world.

While the story may no longer be his own, he had something else that was quite unique. The final autographs Eileen had ever written on the various notes she had left him. And that was the greatest prize of all.

# SIDE TWO

# UPON A PYRAMID

As my dream snapped to a close, I could tell someone was moving about my chambers. But even in my half-awake state, I felt no threat, for I could sense who it was. I felt a warmth upon my cheek and smiled.

Through the remaining clouds of sleep, I heard my love say, "I'm going now."

My eyes opened and Harmii stood there, a thin robe overtop her expedition clothing. She rubbed her hand against the ridges of my skull.

"Where are you going?" I asked, my voice still stricken with disuse from my deep sleep.

"Disturbance at the southern tip of the continent." The soft light of a warm day crept between the gap in the curtain and the door, and the way the light hit her scalp made her appear more elegant than she already was. A goddess of the highest caliber. She could be a model of beauty, worth recognition in the archives. "It's probably just a meteor, but we have to check," she added and slipped on her gauntlet from the stone statue we used as a table.

"Let me go," I said, beginning to sit up from the sleeping stone we shared each night.

Harmii placed her hand on my chest, keeping me in place. "No, no. Talkeet and I can handle it. Besides, you took the last one when I was sick last season. I have to do *some* work around here."

"Talkeet still says that was the worst expedition he's been on. The arctic region of this world is peculiar to say the least," I said with a chuckle.

Harmii rested her cheek against mine. "I'll be back in a couple of days. There are a few samples I want to collect while I'm down in that pocket of the globe anyway."

She stood tall, allowing me to sit upright. "Are you sure you'll be fine?"

"I'm sure." Harmii laughed. "We need someone to keep an eye on our children. They would be offended if one of us didn't bask in the celebrations they arrange."

"I would rather skip such drivel," I said, my face souring.

"One of the many reasons I'm chasing after meteorites." Her sweet laugh warmed my hearts. It was the small things she did that reminded me why I loved her so. "Look at it this way," she added, "it's a distraction from our relief being late with our retrieval."

"I had almost forgotten," I lied. "But to be honest, I've almost come to think of this place as my home," I lied again.

"Not I. I miss the flat plains; I feel boxed in here," Harmii responded as she tightened the clasps of her boots.

I could hear voices coming from the far side of the curtain. No doubt our servant children arriving with our breakfast.

"I do miss home food, though. When we get back, I'm making you the most illustrious feast you've ever had," I told her.

"I'll be there," Harmii said as she began to turn towards the light of the entrance. "We just have to be relieved first."

She smiled at me again, before pulling the curtains away. The orange light immediately shifted to a vibrant yellow. In the distance, the top of the forest canopy could be seen from our raised position atop the stone pyramid. The first of our kind allowed our children to build these structures as gifts in their honour.

"Go forth and create," I said to Harmii as she began to descend the stone steps.

"And also uplift," she replied back, her words flooding past the stone altar in front of our bed chamber. The scent of blood from the sacrifice the evening prior still clung about the air, as did the added layer of stains upon the rocky floor.

The voices of our servants became louder as they came into view, holding rocks with burned meat and wooden planks of fruits. Officially, this breed of children had no name, but several of the holy wanderers had referred to them as "humans," and I felt that name would stick.

---

The primitives bowed before me as I sat upon my golden throne atop the main pyramid.

*Gold*, I thought as a frown formed on my face. *The most useless of trinkets. Yet these natives cherish it. Shower us in it. Where they picked up this fascination with something so trivial is beyond me. We did not put that in their gene pairings.*

I looked down at the bowing crowd, thousands of faces moving off into the distance of the surrounding city. My eyes left them and moved to the smaller pyramid in the distance. Fires burned at its base, and chanting echoing off the stone structures scattered inside the walls.

*Their ritual for the creation day continues*, I thought as I put a fist under my chin and leaned against the armrest. *They are off by a full twenty-nine cycles, which they failed to comprehend when I told them last rotation.*

My eyes scanned the faces as I thought about the prospect of selecting one of them like last year. They all looked the same to me, so I took comfort in the thought that it was truly arbitrary whom I would pick. I waved a hand and the crowd rose. Part two of the ceremony could commence now that I had given my so-called blessing.

The smells of spices entered my nostrils. Truly sickening stuff. I clenched my teeth, knowing that because one of my fore-bearers many rotations prior enjoyed it, the children assumed all of us "gods" wished to partake as well.

*I hope our relief arrives soon, so I can get away from this bland world. I'll miss their mountains, though.*

As the sun started to drift from the centre of the sky, I began to grow apathetic towards the festival's pomp. I stood, deciding that a walk would be the best course of action. I brushed the itchy cloak they had adorned me in to the ground and began my descent down the steps of the structure.

Arriving in the stone courtyard, I could see in my peripherals that my bodyguards had roused themselves from their feast and wandered over. The way these brutes walked reminded me of the chimps we raised them from. I made it to the exit of our compound and passed several towers. My guards began to converse in their archaic dialect as we did so. Their mumblings began to annoy me.

Why our children thought I needed protection was beyond me. I could lift even the largest of them with a single arm, and the gauntlet I wore could fry their primitive brains into boiling mush. But still, the bodyguards followed.

Harmii told me that she had once seen how the guards picked their ranks. It was a brutal blood sport, with the vast number of applicants perishing during the opening night of their arrival. I laughed under my breath as my feet hit the wet grass that marked the end of the so-called holy city. The notion that these primitives considered themselves the best of their species, when they required no additional effort on my part to dispatch, is what caused the laughter to escape my lips.

One of my guards murmured something behind me, and suddenly I found their presence to be unbearable. I raised a fist before making a sign with my fourth and seventh finger. I heard the primitives bow before rising and turning away. I would have preferred to be with my own kind, but short of that, I would rather be alone.

I looked to the sky. A soft rain was brewing and began to make a clicking sound as it splashed against the ridges of my forehead, moving down to my nose. As I walked into the jungle, I let my mind wander.

I crossed a stream and thought of why I volunteered to visit a world such as this. I pulled myself over a downed log and thought of Harmii and the status of her expedition. I moved into a clearing and wondered why my kind had bothered to even make these children. Why alter DNA strands, or experiment on the indigenous life?

While these ideas plagued my mind, the answer to a different question came to me just as I arrived at the centre of a clearing. This had been the first time our experiments had taken hold to such great effect. All the others died in the operating chalice or upon the nursery chrysalis. Our meddling had never come this far and our philosophers wanted to see where such a gift bestowed on another species would lead.

My thoughts were interrupted when I dragged my foot upon a hard surface. Annoyed by the slight discomfort, I looked down, expecting to see a rock. But, to my surprise, my eyes met a grey-blue object. It looked like a scale or shell of some sort.

I adjusted my robes and bent down, prying the object from the hardened dirt. The sun gleamed off the object as I held it in the air with both hands, my golden-eyed reflection gazing back at me.

I shook the item and realised it was hollow. I turned the egg-shaped object end over end until I observed a small nub at the top of it. I pulled on the irregularity and felt a click as it came free.

Nothing happened.

Letting out a grunt of annoyance, I moved my face closer to

the opening. A scent escaped its confined depths and I grimaced at such a wretched smell. I struggled to classify the scent, but I could identify synthetic undertones about it, which proved this object could not be natural. I coughed, careful to hold the object far from my face as I did so.

After several moments, I collected myself and looked at the peculiar item in my outstretched hand. In all my years, I had never seen anything quite like it. Despite the odd fauna and flora of this world, I knew it was unlike anything else here. Clearly it was a container of some sort, but what could it be used to hold? What would cause such a foul odor?

I lowered the object to the ground and wondered if perhaps our children were capable of creating anything even remotely close to this.

As I straightened up, I felt my back tense, aware of just how exposed I was. The sense of being watched sprang over me and became the only thing I could think about.

I spun around and looked at every possible spot where something could be lurking. Only the surrounding clearing dared to gaze back at me. No animals, no movement; just me, alone in such an alien environment.

I gulped and felt the feelers in my throat tense up at just how far I had ventured from the city. In my reverie I had walked for over an hour. I looked to the horizon and saw the sun was getting close to dipping behind the treeline. I began to hyperventilate as I realised I was hours away from my teammates.

*Something placed this object here and it was not one of us*, I thought before my mind turned to Harmii. *Does her investigation at the tip of the continent have anything to do with this?*

It was then that I dropped the container to the ground. I ran towards the holy city, not stopping until my top set of lungs burned and my lower set shrivelled in fatigue.

Panting for breath, I leaned against a tree and gathered my thoughts. I started to second guess myself. Perhaps I misremembered the object? Maybe if I went back and looked at it again, I would realise it had been something natural—a type of fruit that had gone to rot or peculiar stone that had amassed some stagnant water inside it. But that smell! And the odd colour of the material. I clicked my teeth in anger at not having the forethought to bring the object with me.

I walked the rest of the way, only arriving at the holy city once the sun had vanished and the still of the night had swallowed up this part of the planet.

The guards at the entrance snapped up from their spots around the fire, their spears raised and visceral grunts escaping their mouths. Upon recognising their master, they drove their foreheads to the dirt.

I moved around them and entered the city. Several small groups of our children still lingered here and there, but they appeared not to notice me. I began my assent up the steps of the pyramid, my thoughts lingering on the object in the clearing.

I entered my sleeping quarters and moved over to a small case tucked behind my resting slab. I manipulated the finger lock, stopping when I heard the security strips connect. I flipped open the case and pulled out one of the survey drones. I changed the settings on the side and set the coordinates to my best approximation of where Harmii's investigation site would be. I then changed a parameter in its settings for it to seek out any of our scout ships nearby.

I leaned against the resting slab and recorded a message, informing her of what I had found. I also asked for her to be careful and to return to the city.

Even as I spoke the words, I realised how paranoid I sounded. Our civilization had ventured into countless star systems and investigated more than a hundred habitable worlds, and we had never come across another civilization that had evolved passed the third phase, let alone the forty-first needed to obtain space travel. Still, I uploaded the message into the drone's systems and moved to the entrance of the pyramid.

As I raised the device over my head, I contemplated sending

a far-cast message from my mind to Harmii directly, but quickly dismissed this idea. I worried of the repercussions, as I knew the signal had a tendency to disturb the natives, something I could ill afford since I was alone to police them.

I tossed the drone up and watched as it took flight into the moonlit sky. I was well aware it would take all night to reach its destination, but I was comforted by the fact that upon receiving it, Harmii would return to me.

The dreams I had that night were vivid, and with that clarity came horrific motifs. Eyes and faceless entities followed me everywhere I dared to venture.

When I finally awoke from that sweat-soaked coma, I squinted at the bright light that seeped between the doorway curtain and the wall. I arose and informed a servant to summon the ape that they had selected as a priest.

When the aging child arrived, I asked if there had been any reports of movement in the trees or any odd sightings by the gatherers.

His reply came in a broken subdialect of my language. I shuddered as he tripped over phrasing and was thankful not all our children attempted to butcher my language like this one was. The message of his answer was clear, however: No sightings of anything other than animals for the hunt.

I dismissed him before grabbing a cloth sack that hung from the ears of a statue near the entrance. I slung the pack over my shoulder and pulled open the curtain.

As I moved out to the podium, the entire city bowed. I waved my hand to free them from such a useless custom. I looked to the sky, hoping to see the survey drone, as I was eager to receive Harmii's reply, for it alone would prove that she and Talkeet were okay. I sighed as my gaze was met by only a blue sky and puffy white clouds.

My face soured and looked to the green of the foliage that surrounded the city like a tightening noose. I could not shake the feeling that I was no longer alone with our creations. That object I had discovered had not been of this world, nor any we had visited, for that matter.

I shook my head and begun my descent of the stairs. I was going to investigate that clearing again, and now that I had a full day ahead of me, I could search in more detail.

The walk through the bush was exactly as it had been the day prior. I was careful to retrace my steps, even if I had only been half paying attention the last time I trudged this path. I was able to pass the same overturned logs, knotted vines, and rushing rivers.

Before I knew it, I was at the clearing. The sense of dread rose through me once more as I stepped into it. With perseverance and determination, I continued.

I was quick to find the object laying in the same spot where I had cast it aside yesterday. I placed it in the sack that I had brought from my sleep chambers and focused my gaze on the surrounding area, paying particular attention to the contours of the grass. While my eyes had been searching for footprints or other containers, what I saw surprised me.

I observed several spots in the clearing lacking grass entirely. The missing sections were all oval and identical in shape and equally spaced apart. While common in my world for nature to work in grids, I knew that was a near impossibility on this planet.

I roamed over to the closest spot and ran my fingers over the blades of grass that outlined the oval. They were intact, no sign of burn nor cut, but I could see stress marks upon the dirt in each divot. Something heavy had been placed there.

It occurred to me then that I was standing in the spot where a ship had landed.

All my paranoia and fears became justified in that moment. Something else had visited this world—and recently, judging by how fresh these oval markings looked. It was not outside the realm of possibility that whatever these beings were had also caused the disturbance that Harmii was investigating.

I began to clear my mind in preparation to send a message via far-cast, but stopped. *I have already sent a message using the drone and she would no doubt have already received it*, I thought as I scanned the clearing once more for good measure. *If I send this message now, I would just be repeating myself.*

I shook my head, realising that I cared little about sending the same message twice. I had to be sure she was safe.

With considerable focus, I sent the message and hoped the distance from the holy city was great enough that it would not turn the population there into a frenzy. I felt the message leave my mind and awaited her response.

I waited. And waited. And waited.

No reply ever came.

It was then I began to panic. Harmii had always replied to my far-cast messages with little delay. She should have broken the silence by now. Especially since she knew I would not use that method of communication without good reason.

Something was wrong.

I left the clearing with haste. I deduced that I would get to the city by midday, and from there, I would pilot the sole remaining scout craft. If I used the imbedded trackers I could fly to Harmii's last known location and hold her in my arms again. Then we were leaving this world, research vessel or not. Somehow, we were leaving. I just needed to figure that last part out.

As I approached the jewel that was the holy city, my knees ached like they never had before. But while that did not slow me, something else stopped me in my tracks entirely.

The entrance was unguarded, and that had never happened before.

*Rain, blistering heat, day or night—they have always been there*, I thought as I looked to the ground, seeing no sign of struggle. *Where have they gone?*

With a cautiousness to my steps, I entered the city. My fingers tapped my gauntlet in a show of nerves. I passed empty huts with no sign of our children anywhere. It wasn't until I rounded a corner and my eyes wandered to the precipice of the pyramid that my mouth fell open in horrified awe.

One of the clouds had taken on a trapezoidal shape, jutting down lower than the rest. It appeared too clean, too perfect in its contours. I knew immediately that this was not a cloud at all, but a ship of some sort, and it did not belong to any of my kin.

I took a quickened step forward, but stopped again as my eyes gravitated to the base of the structure. There, all our children knelt, heads to the dirt. Their murmuring calls of devotion now met my ears. The same chants they had given to my kind for generations.

Upon the steps of the pyramid, I saw three figures standing over them. My lips curled in disgust as I made out the hideous features of the invader. Elongated snouts. Jagged teeth escaping twisted mouths. Bronze-coloured eyes and green scaly skin, as well as an extra set of arms jutting from the side of their torsos.

*Another intelligent species…*

I moved to step back, and it was then one of the beings looked in my direction. What should have been a historical moment of cross species contact was only met with fear. A screeching sound escaped its lips.

I saw several of our children raise their heads and look over their shoulders. I used this opportunity to shout a command, the holy word for "seize and sacrifice," as I pointed to the invaders.

Several of the children looked between me and the beings that stood over them. They returned to their worshipping chants with little more than a blink.

*No loyalty in apes,* I thought, taking another step back, noting that not a single one of my children lay slain in the congregation. It occurred to me that these foreigners had come and not even one of my children had so much as raised a finger in protest.

I contemplated running but remembered the words of an instructor on my first expedition. *Gods never run,* he had said.

I stepped forward, newfound courage rising from some previously unknown crevasse in my hearts. I would seize these beasts, and using my gauntlets, make short work of them. Then I would teach these primitives the consequences of bowing to a false prophet.

I managed to take one more step forward before one of the invaders sprung down the steps of the pyramid with an unnatural speed. Faster than I had ever been able to descend those steep stairs. I froze and it raised a jagged black object with one hand. As the device was pointed in my direction, I felt a tightening in my chest. A moment of excruciating pain overcame me just before I felt six of my ribs snap, leaving me in agony.

I keeled over in pain, my mind struggling to understand what sort of weapon system could do what was being done to me. A being as strong as I, as *perfect* as I, reduced to a shrivelling worm.

I spat up a crystallised blackened soup and I knew something inside me had been pierced. As the pain continued to swell, I could feel another set of my ribs giving way. With all my strength, I dove to my left into an alleyway between two stone buildings. While the tightening ceased, the dagger-edge sensation of punctured organs and shattered bone only increased with the impact against the packed dirt.

I stumbled forward, closing my eyes to activate the emergency stim pack embedded along my spine. The adrenaline and painkillers flowed forth immediately and made the pain almost bearable. I coughed up another volley of thick blood, spraying it along the walls of the alley.

I regained my speed and moved forward, hearing the hissing sounds change in both tone and direction. These creatures were calling to each other, and I could detect excitement in their chittering calls. I was making a good hunt for them.

The chanting from my former children had ceased as well,

and I could hear their voices getting closer. While I could not understand their words, I doubted this was the time they were coming to defend my honour.

I ran down the alleyway and took a left down a side path that snaked towards the city's stone wall. From there, I took another left and ran between the huts and out through the main gate. The shouts of children behind me ensured they had seen me double back, but the echo of these calls led me to believe I had a fair-sized lead on them.

*Fickle, fickle apes,* I thought, as I ran around the perimeter of the city. My goal was to get to the far end where the last scout craft was located. *We raise them from nothing, and they forsake us at the first sign of something new. How they worshipped us for hundreds of rotations around their feeble star. Swapping allegiances like a snake sheds its skin.*

I looked to the sky and could see the false cloud was still overhead. Either the invaders on the ground had not communicated with it yet, or they had something else in store for me.

I moved to the edge of the wall and passed the western entrance of the city. My gauntlet was primed in case any of my former children or the invaders dared to get in my way. With luck, the coast was clear.

I looked to my right into the treeline. From there I could see a small, spiked craft. Its hull was the same scaley blue as the object that now jostled in the sack I wore. I studied it for a moment to ensure no hostile was present before moving on.

As I reached my scout craft behind the pyramid, the pain in my shredded organs was quickly becoming unbearable again. I opened the hatch with both palm scanners and jumped inside. I primed the engine, allowing the guidance system to lock onto the locations of the other two scout ships somewhere on the edge of the southern continent.

As it did so, I reached behind the chair and into the storage area and pulled out a small cylinder, guzzling the liquid inside. Tossing aside the empty canister, I proceeded to seize a container of black gel. I lifted my cloak and applied the medication liberally to my chest and sides. The mix of healing drugs made me feel groggy and more light-headed than I already was.

A light press on my pulverised ribs did all the waking up I needed.

To ensure I did not lose consciousness on my voyage, I grabbed a package of morning powder and slammed back double the recommended dosage. The guidance system locked onto the signal of Harmii's ship, and I activated the engines.

As my craft left the ground, I switched on the observer camouflage that was designed to keep the ship hidden while we studied primitive species from above. My ship was now invisible to the naked eye, and I hopped that the vessel in the sky didn't possess scanners able to track me.

As I fled from the holy city, my eyes stayed locked on the trapezoidal cloud above me. I expected a payload of ordnance to come screaming my way, but to my thankful surprise, the alien ship stayed floating in place. No doubt wondering where I had gone.

---

The journey to the southern tip of the continent was entirely uneventful as I maxed out my scout ship's drives. My eyes moved between scanners and the ships exterior cameras constantly, as I looked to see if I was being followed. I had seen nothing for hours and had initially been thankful, but that thanks quickly changed to a slew of worried emotions as my ship neared the spot that Harmii's ship beacon was located. It had not moved since I had taken flight.

I wished to contact her again with far-cast, but I was worried they could track it somehow. After all, they had only approached when I had used it before. I knew the link between the two events was most likely coincidental, but the idea lingered and kept me from clearing my mind.

After one final switch from the rear cameras to the forward set, I could see a smoke plume on the horizon. My hearts began to thump against my shattered ribs and I knew that I would be flying over the wreck of one of my companions.

I moved over to the spot and set my ship to hover. Below I could see the scattered remains of a scout craft below.

Just as my grief began to swell, my eyes glimpsed the scanners on the console in front of me. The beacon marking Harmii's ship was another grid away.

With newfound purpose, I accelerated and left the remains of Talkeet's ship behind. *Harmii's alive,* I thought, my hands trembling on the steering controls. *She's alive, I know it.*

I completed a pass over the next grid area, but the trees were too thick to see her ship below. Another circle of the area resulted in spotting a small gap in the foliage canopy and I began my landing sequence.

I visualised moving to the scene of the beacon, seeing Harmii using her ship as cover, a gauntlet pointing at me. Her eyes glowing as she recognised me and the two of us fleeing together. My mind skipped over the details of how I would fit her inside my single seat craft, but that was not important; finding her safe and unharmed was the only detail I cared to focus on.

As my landing gear made contact with the jungle floor, I exited the opening hatch. With my gauntlet charged to maximum pulse, I ran in the direction of the beacon. I sprinted for several minutes until I came across the cold grey-brown metals of the scout ship. It looked undamaged, but the cockpit canopy was open. I gingerly stuck my head in the opening and saw the flight seat was empty. I turned around, my mind beginning to fracture at Harmii's absence.

I moved behind the craft and could see several small machines had been deployed, no doubt part of Harmii's expedition to uncover what was causing the disturbances. I looked to the foliage ceiling above me and expressed my will to the universe. I wanted to see Harmii again.

As I lowered my head, it was then I saw the whites of the eyes surrounding me from between the trees. I turned and watched as a formation of my children approached from all directions. They looked more feral than the ones that lived in the holy city, but we had elevated them all just the same. They recognised one of their gods.

"Help me find her," I said in a simplified variation of my language.

I was a fool to think they were here to help. As they ignored my command and continued forward, I knew the invaders had gotten to them as well.

I pivoted and moved towards my ship. A mammoth of an ape stepped out in front of me. His club was held above his head to batter my skull in. I raised my gauntlet, making contact with his chest. The beast crumpled as its brain bubbled into mush and leaked out its ears.

Two other primitives who had begun to intercept me ceased moving as they saw the brain matter pouring out of their relative's head.

I struggled to understand how the invaders had turned all the children against me in such a short amount of time. A city was one thing, but all of them on a continent? Impossible.

*What of the ones elsewhere?* my inner voice asked as I moved off into the trees.

As I reached my scout ship I felt the burning in my organs again. The pain was so severe that I could not pull myself into the open canopy. As I fell to the ground, I knew that the invaders had me in their sites. I lay there, convulsing with violent spasms that sent my limbs flailing.

I felt something pop in my chest and then tasted blood on my tongue. I could now see the faces of my former children looming overhead. They gazed down at me with blank looks, like I was nothing more than a dying insect.

Movement in the sky above forced me to look past them. The clouds looked odd and then I saw the trapezoidal shape, and it was growing nearer. Then a blue-scaled object began to descend, shedding the cloud like a layer of skin.

---

To my surprise, I awoke.

The darkness of death—or near death, I suppose—was blinding, crippling, and most importantly, endless. This went against everything I had heard from the philosophers. They had all stared into the afterlife, guided by herbs from deep beneath our second moon. Upon their return from their metaphysical journeys, they all spoke of being welcomed among the gods for our service. For continuing their work in the creation and uplifting of life.

But what I saw here led me to believe there was no plan.

As I lay there on a cold hard slab, looking at the darkening sky, it was this notion that I thought the most about. Not the sting of my ruptured organs. Not my failure of finding Harmii. Not even the humbling idea that we were no longer the only intelligent race in the universe.

No, my mind lingered on the irrefutable fact that we had been sold a lie.

I sent out a shallow exhale in grief towards the sliver of a moon beginning to creep into view from behind the clouds.

It was then my grogginess dissipated enough that I heard the chanting.

I realised now that I was upon the pyramid, the one reserved for us, the uplifters. I looked to my right, down at the crowd, and in my peripherals I could see the blood-stained altar I laid upon.

It was then I recognised the chanting. The same one they shouted for the sacrifices.

In my weakened state, I rolled my head back to return my gaze to the night sky. But the moon was lost behind something else, for one of the invaders stood over me. Its green scales seemed to ripple in the night as those bronze-coloured eyes gazed down at me. The black slit of its pupils narrowed. I expected it to mock me then, to call me a false god, unworthy of the gifts our children had given us, but its mouth stayed sealed.

As the creature raised a jagged stone knife high above its head, the chanting ceased. I knew my time had come.

In the eternity between the knife beginning to lower and the piercing of my abdomen, I focused on what I could see upon looking at the end. I was glad there would be no gods there to judge us. For judge us they would, and their judgment would be swift.

We weren't creators; we were meddlers. Tinkerers. Bored infants with too much time on our hands. Too confident in our self-imposed place and role in the universe.

I welcomed the darkness. At least it had never lied about what it was.

In my last moments, I used all my energy to send out a far-cast into the depths of space, hoping to warn my kin of what had happened here. As I felt the blade slip inside me, my eyes widened, and I opened myself up as a receiver for millions of communications. The wet sensation slithered across my chest, and I heard the cheering crowd reel into mindless screams of agony as the far-cast signals entered their craniums.

The messages that spun around inside my head were remnant pleas for help, and I could sense they were all that remained of voices long extinguished.

As the darkness came for me, it brought with it the crippling anguish that this had not been an isolated attack by the invaders, but a calculated genocide.

# THE TRAIN STATION

The locomotive roamed through the countryside. It blew its whistle at the empty hills, steel wheels rumbling over the track as it listened to its roar reflect off the shimmering lakes. On and on, the train wandered by into the days ahead. The coal burned hot, and the black smoke billowed up though its stack and into the calm skies above.

It did this until it decided it was time to stop.

The train pulled into a town with no name, for the people aboard the train had not named it yet. There was a sharp screech as the brakes were applied and the train gently glided up to the platform that sat waiting to receive its next guests, its next caregivers.

This platform had been alone a long while with only the summer heat to keep it warm and the winter frosts to comfort it. But now it was alone no longer, for family had arrived. Hundreds of relatives it had yet to meet. The station only hoped they would be staying a while longer than the last group had.

The train car doors opened, and the travellers began their disorganised exit. Some were ready to begin exploring and mapping out the area immediately. The vast majority however were weary from the journey.

"It's quaint," said the mother. "But beautiful."

"There's not much to this town," said the daughter.

"That's because we haven't built it up yet," replied the father as he heaved two suitcases down the short steps of the train car.

"Why did the last people not build more?" asked the son. "Why did they leave it so small?"

The father placed the cases on the concrete platform and knelt, looking into his son's eyes. "Gordon," he said, "we don't know anything about the people that lived here before us. There could have been only a few of them, or they may have only been here for a short time. We don't know and we won't ever know."

"Why can't we meet them?" the daughter asked as she danced to imaginary music, using the wind to twist this way and that.

"We will never meet the ones ahead of us, nor behind. That's the way it has always been."

"But I don't want to build a new town," the son said. "I liked the old one. I want to go back."

Copious amounts of travellers moved along the platform and headed through the gap in the hedges, towards the shabby little town at the bottom of the hill. The train was nearly empty now.

The father ruffled his son's hair. "You were born in that town, and we were lucky that last time we got to stay as long as we did." He looked off down the tracks from which they had come. "It's not normally like that." The father blinked, before returning his gaze to his son. "I understand that you miss it, but believe me, it will pass. Your mother and I have seen dozens of towns."

"Why can't we go back?" the son cried, tears forming at the corners of his eyes.

The mother shared a look with her husband before turning to her son and saying, "The train only moves forward, honey. We can't go back from once we came."

The father hugged his son. "This town will be our new home. Just wait. I promise it will feel like it soon enough."

The train sat dormant on the platform and watched as the inhabitants settled into their new homes. At first, progress was slow. The two-street town had little to offer in terms of tools and resources. The people, having been out of their routine of work since boarding the steam engine, were less than enthused to venture back up to the station. The notion of hauling their saws and axes and pullies and ropes from the storage cars at the back of the train was a task that sounded quite unpleasant indeed.

But after a while, slowly but surely, that is exactly what they did. They turned the dust-covered roads to cobblestone. Transformed the shabby cabins to wonderful neighbourhoods. They farmed the nearby fields, and mined the tunnel system that rested out past the creek. Through hard work and determination, they turned the small town into a cozy village.

One day, several seasons after the train had stopped, little Gordon sat upon a wooden bench on the platform. He had been in the middle of celebrating his eleventh birthday when he decided to venture in this direction. He looked at the train with great sadness.

Gordon sat there for a long while until his father ran up the hill, shouting his name.

"Gordon?" his father called again after no response, his voice much closer now, rising through the bushes.

Upon seeing his son, he said, "Gordon! What are you doing up here? It's your birthday! Come back; we were about to grab the cake."

"Dad, why do we do this?" Gordon asked, as he looked at the train's perfect steel architecture. There was no sign of rust or mud on its frame; the paint was still as shiny as it had ever been.

"What do you mean?" the father replied, looking around the platform. "You mean take the train?"

"No," Gordon replied as he played with the strings of his sweater. "I understand that." He looked to the tracks as they moved off into the distance. Forward. Always forward to the next unseen station, towards the future. "We can never go backwards, only forwards, but—" Gordon stopped speaking and hugged his father as he sat down beside him. "Why do we build all this when we are just going to have to leave anyway?"

"Who said we are leaving?" the father asked as he put his arm around his son.

"Hanna and her friends said so last night. They said that many people in town think the train will move soon. It will blow its whistle and that will be it." He paused, trying hard to fight the tears. "They said that since we were in the last town for so many years, it won't happen twice. Hanna said she was surprised we've been here for as long as we have even now."

"Your sister can be … insensitive at times," the father replied, looking down the opposite end of the tracks.

"But why do we bother?" Gordon continued. "Why do we build so much only to leave it all behind and then repeat the process when we move again?"

The father looked down the tracks to the cities he had left behind in his life. "We build them so the next train of people that comes can enjoy what we have built and then build off it to make it better. Just like the train ahead of us does. They build until the whistle comes and then they must leave, just like we will."

"And why do we listen to the train?"

The father glanced to the steam engine for a moment before looking down at his boy. "We must always listen to the train, Gordon."

"But how does it know when it is time to leave? How does it know when—"

"The train always knows, and you must always trust that it knows what's best for us."

Despite what many people in the village said, the train did not call that spring, nor the summer after. Not when the autumn that stripped the trees came, or the winter with its blizzards. It did not call until the boy named Gordon turned eighteen.

The blare of the whistle echoed through the settlement and into the hills behind. It moved through the mines and up to the logging cabins. People in the midst of their labour looked up. Marriage ceremonies ceased mid sermon. Babies cried and children hugged their mother's dresses, as they had never heard such a sound.

The people of the village retreated from their tasks and threw their valuables into luggage that had long been gathering dust in their closets. Meals were left uneaten, books left unread, artwork left half painted. Everyone knew they needed to get to the train.

Gordon ran down the road with his luggage in one hand and his sister's hand in the other. While they were both adults, their father kept calling from ahead, "Stay together!"

"No one gets separated," the mother called back, looking over her shoulder. "No one stays behind."

They passed through the village centre, prompting Gordon to experience a wave of nostalgia for all the stores and businesses in which he had spent so much of his life. The barbershop where he had gotten his first and subsequent fifty haircuts. The school where he spent the majority of his waking childhood hours. The small printing shop where he worked his first job two summers prior. The theater where he met his first love, and the park behind it where he had his first kiss. All the memories came back to him, each blaring a train whistle of their own.

"I don't want to leave," Gordon said from the back of the group. "I like it here. My whole life was—is—here." He began to loosen his grip on his older sister's hand, but Hanna squeezed tighter.

The father looked back, narrowly avoiding colliding with a slower family as they moved up the hill towards the platform. "No, Gordon, you can't stay. We must move forward."

Gordon sunk his heels into the dirt and Hanna lost her grip. The family turned and looked back at Gordon.

"Moving on is never easy, but we must." His mother stepped forward to embrace her child, but Gordon pulled away.

The train whistle grew more impatient with its calls.

"We can't be left behind," the father said. "The train will not wait."

"I want to live my life here. I want to see all it has to offer. I'm not done here yet."

"When the train says it's time to go, we must go," the father said, his voice a compassionate call as the train shouted once more.

The streets were now empty, with only the single family remaining at the base of the hill.

"I will carry you," the father said. "I will if I must." He dropped his luggage. "You don't think I felt the same way before, when I was young? When all I had ever known was one place? Twenty-two years, all in one city."

"You did?" Gordon asked, as he felt his mother hug him from the side.

"Of course," the father said. "I had lived in that city my entire life to that point. I was heartbroken. Devastated. But I knew I had to go." The wind blew a slew of colourful leaves across the boulevard. The father stepped forward and continued, "I knew it was time to leave and I'm glad I did. For the train took me to so many new places; so many new experiences. It took me to meet your mother, it took me to meet my passion, and most importantly, it took me to meet Hanna and you." The father stepped forward, his hand extended for his child to take. "Please, Son."

Gordon gripped his father's hand and felt his feet move from under him. There was no time to savour the moment, as the family turned and moved up the hill towards the platform.

Gordon's eyes stayed locked on the train. He wholeheartedly expected to see it shunt forward, leaving them behind. He recalled then all of the conversations he had overheard about the train and suddenly realised that to be left behind might be a fate worse than death. He squeezed his father's hand tight, hoping he would not be the one responsible for his family missing the train.

They made it to the platform as the locomotive sat there in its majesty. The family clamoured into the nearest car, huffing and puffing as they did so. The father turned and hugged his children, the mother securing the door behind them.

The family found a window cabin and stowed their luggage under the small mattresses that would serve as their beds for the journey ahead. All except Gordon, who stood at the closed door, his eyes locked on the place where he had spent his formative years. Each brick, stone, and tree held a lifetime of memories.

The train let out one final whistle that echoed through the empty village, before the sound of grinding metal rang out behind the wheels. The train lurched forward, and Gordon hung his head before heading off to his family's room.

———

The train rumbled on for day upon day, and night upon night. It stopped at many cities and towns, and each time the train's inhabitants disembarked and built a life for themselves. But it never stopped as long as it had when Gordon was ten years old.

Gordon was celebrating his eighty-ninth birthday when the train decided to stop again. He was escorted out of the car by his young grandchildren, as his own children were gathering the luggage.

"Look, Grandpa," little Isaac said. "This city is so nice, and so big!"

Gordon looked in awe at the city that stretched on towards the horizon. He savoured the site before saying, "I recognise this place." He gripped Isaac's hand. "It has changed, but I recognise it."

He remembered the spots where the library and film house had been. The masonry shop where his father had worked and the café where Hanna had tended the register. The names of the stores were different now, but the buildings were the same. Tears filled Gordon's eyes.

"What's the matter, Grandpa?" Isaac asked, and the rest of the family moved towards him to see what was wrong.

Gordon reached out and patted the side of the majestic train. "They said we could never go back, but that's not true. We can always come back, but only when the time is right."

# THE BONFIRE

I sat shotgun in dad's pickup truck as we bumped down the dirt road to the gathering that marked the end of harvest. The idea of attending my first bonfire brought the butterflies in my stomach to a jittery flight. I felt like I was living the first day in a new chapter of my life.

I fumbled with my cherry-blonde braid, and he must have sensed that I was nervous.

"It's a big responsibility, coming out here," he said in his usual drawl. "Especially at your age."

"I know, Pop," I replied, looking to him. His plaid shirt was rolled up at the sleeves, revealing burly forearms.

"I know you're younger than most of the kids who come to the ceremony," he gripped the steering wheel, "but, well, you're my daughter and I was your age when my old man—er, your grandpop—took me to my first bonfire."

"I know," I replied with a certain exuberance. "You said that at breakfast this morning."

"Yes, um, yes I did. What I'm trying to say is, this bonfire here is an important part of our community, and I know you're old enough to understand. Hell, no child of mine is born no simpleton." His voice was stern, but he rubbed my head with his mitt of a hand while the other still clutched the steering wheel.

I could see the dirt pluming behind us as we scooted down the road. The sun shrunk low on the horizon behind us, turning the hills in the distance to a shadowy pink.

He looked at me, watching me stare out the window before saying, "What'cha thinking about there, sweetie? Are you nervous?"

"No, Pop," I replied as I looked down at the chipped red polish on my nails. "Just excited."

"It will be quite the experience. Something you won't be forgetting, neither."

Recently I had wondered if my father had wished he had been given a son instead of me. I don't know what makes someone think that, but such things did cross my mind on occasion. Either way, he never showed his displeasure in me, and I never complained when he gave me what the city folk called "boy chores." I always helped him in the field and held tools for him while he fixed the tractor and always chopped wood with him when that time of year came. Tasks everyone should know, I reckoned, boy or girl. Those city boy sissies wouldn't grow up to be men, not a real man like my pop. I appreciated him showing me those things.

Father pointed his finger over top of the steering wheel like he was calling his shot, just like that Babe feller did. "There she is."

I followed his finger with my eyes into the dusty twilight. There it was indeed. The small embers signalled the humble beginnings of what would become the towering bonfire. A small congregation, mostly boys, crowded around the piled pallets that served as its base.

Them being boys didn't startle me any. No, sir. I could take 'em. I knew if anyone spoke ill of me being there, Pop would throw 'em all in the dirt, no if, ands, or buts.

We pulled off the main road and onto Uncle Jim's property.

The man wasn't really my uncle, despite me calling him that my whole life. I only found out that detail last year, but it was just easier to still refer to him as such.

The wheat in the field had all been harvested, and for miles I could see the golden nubs of what remained. Even in its humble beginning stage, the bonfire looked like a beacon casting its light across a million gold coins.

In the mirror beside me, headlights caught my eye. Several other trucks had turned off the main road and entered the property as well. Tonight looked like it would be quite the turn out. I didn't have anything to compare it to, but a lot of people is a lot of people.

Pop parked the truck beside the Wilson's rusting Dodge and got out. He shook hands with several folks I saw at church most Sundays.

I exited the vehicle and walked over to join Pop. The conversations stopped as Mr. Wilson and two others with him stared down at me, a nervous shuffling between them.

"She's young, Mike. Real young," Mr. Wilson said, adjusting his ball cap. "My boy is thirteen and this is his first one." He gestured to the boy who stood behind him, nearly as tall as he was, which wasn't saying much.

"She'll be fine," Pop said with a calm tone as he placed a hand on my shoulder. "They don't make 'em tougher than my daughter. No way, no how."

"Alright…" Mr. Wilson said with a shrug, fishing a cigarette out of his breast pocket.

Pop took me by the hand and led me through the growing crowd. "Don't listen to them, sweetie. And don't listen to your mother neither. This is important." His eyes darted around for a moment before he looked down at me and added, "Well, listen to her every other time, just not this once." He winked, and brought me to the front of the crowd. "Have to get a good view for your first time—you gotta remember it."

I could feel the excitement building inside me. As the bonfire grew with every snap of wood and pop of ember, so did my anticipation.

"Oh, you brought Mary-Beth along," a voice from behind said, prompting both Pop and I to turn. It was Uncle Jim. "Excellent," he added before spitting a wad of chewing tobacco into the dirt under his dusty cowboy boots. "Excellent is as excellent does."

He smiled and shook Pop's hand, then looked to me. "My little Sarah enjoyed her first one last year. She'll be around shortly, just helping the missus get coffee and biscuits together for the after meeting." He spat out another wad. "Yes, indeed, Sarah was scared last year. Will you be scared, hun?"

"No, sir," I said with as much bravado as I could muster, but I could hear the tinge of unease in my voice.

"That a girl," Uncle Jim said, rubbing my head affectionately. "Exactly. Nothing to be afraid of."

"Tough as a bull and twice as ferocious," Pop added, looking down at me. I could see the pride in his eyes.

"Well, I have to tend to the fire. You two enjoy yourselves tonight," Uncle Jim said as he walked past us. I hadn't seen the man this excited since he won big at poker a few years back.

I felt the cool breeze drift up the rolled cuffs of my jeans and move up the back of my sweater. I shivered and put my hands in my pockets as I looked back at the road in the distance. I noticed the sun was nearly gone now and so too were the headlights. The road was empty.

I turned back as the sounds of the fire increased. I could see the bonfire was devouring its wooden base, the pallets and logs buckling into blackened smolders. Uncle Jim moved to the scoop of his nearby tractor and tossed several logs around the base, whistling as he did so. With the assistance of two other men, he heaved a giant tree trunk, roots and all, on top of the flames.

As the heat sprung out of the fire with gusto, it became the spectacle that I had been promised. Its light shone up and brightened the freshly darkened countryside.

Uncle Jim stepped back and reached into his back pocket, retrieving a little black book. He cleared his throat as he turned to face the crowd. He began to read some of the words from a passage of the text. Some of the words sounded familiar to what the preacher would say on Sundays, but most did not.

As he read, the crowd joined in. The heat of the fire grew, chasing the cold breeze away.

I looked to my right and through the crowd I could see Mr. Wilson standing next to the line of parked trucks, talking to another fella. This stranger wore a cowboy hat and was leaning against the door of a jacked-up GMC. I admired it, seeing it was fitted with lightbars on the front and top. It looked like it was not built for farming but for searching. Or *hunting* might be a better word.

I looked to Mr. Wilson and squinted through the dark to see he had fanned out a series of bills and was handing the stranger a wad of them. The man accepted the money before adjusting his hat. As he fisted the dollars into his back pocket, he looked up at me. Our eyes met, and even from such a distance, I felt the chill in them. I snapped my head forward and looked at the growing flames.

The fire burned brighter and brighter as Uncle Jim read passage after passage. The crackling of the logs and Pop standing tall beside me filled me with a calm that only came a few times in one's life, I reckoned. It made me forget all about the man and those chilling, empty eyes.

Uncle Jim continued to read, and I could see some of the older children getting nervous. Some clinging to their fathers, others whispering anxiously to each other. These were boys that were two, some even three years my senior, and they were scared.

*Pansies, all of them,* I thought as I watched the flames grow higher and higher into the star-speckled sky.

Uncle Jim spoke louder to combat the sounds of the roaring fire. He was nearly yelling the words now.

As we stood in the beacon of light in the middle of the dark countryside, I felt as if I could hear something crackling in the fire. Not tinder, mind you, but something … else. Then I heard it for certain.

The bonfire was speaking back.

Some of the other children shrieked and whined as the voice repeated Uncle Jim's passages before going off on its own.

It was then I saw the cowboy hat-wearing stranger pull something wrapped in sheets from the bed of his jacked-up truck. I watched as the object thumped down in the dirt before Mr. Wilson bent down to help him move it closer. As they dragged the covered object towards the fire, I could see it was shaped like a man, and the way they handled it told me that whoever it had been was no longer living.

They tossed the body into the fire and the voice in the flames began to gurgle in delight. Several of the children turned tail and ran off into the night. The looks on their parents' faces reeked of embarrassment.

But not my dad. He looked down at me with his familiar smile and I could tell he was the proudest parent who ever lived. I stood tall then, for I wasn't scared. I had my pop with me, and I knew he loved me.

# A CHANGING OF THE GUARD

"You know, I never thought when I was hired that I would be part of the last class of humans to accept the badge," Donaldson said, blowing his cigarette smoke into the air. He watched as it disappeared into the fan blades above.

"Remember when the hiring freeze was *temporary*?" Hudson mumbled, as he fiddled with the battery of his lighter, eying a group of expensively dressed business types who stood at the far end of the smoking room.

"Longest hiring freeze for any organisation, I would bet," Donaldson replied, savoring the nicotine substitute before quickly adding, "I'm gonna miss these chats."

"Hey, it's not like we're dying; just unemployed," Hudson said with a thin smile.

"When I first took the job all those years ago, I would have considered the two mutually exclusive," Donaldson said, dropping the remnants of his cigarette to the concrete floor. "But they just don't need frontline humans anymore."

Hudson rubbed the sleeve of his uniform. Though faded from hundreds of washes, the blue and gold Arzonian Border Protection Agency patch glowed up at him. "I knew the writing was on the wall when the uniform supply store closed two years ago." He chuckled. "Down for maintenance... The government always had the best jokes."

"They were trying anything to make us quit, weren't they?"

Hudson nodded as he reminisced on days gone by before fishing out a package of cigarettes and offering the open container to Donaldson. "Well, they could have tried harder. But we hung on." He looked out an observation window as a disembarking ship spooled up its engines, dousing the smoking room in a warm blue as it did. "I heard they are serving cake at the end of our shift," he added, as the ship accelerated off into space.

Donaldson took one of the cigarettes and placed it in his mouth. "Really? I didn't hear anything." His eyes moved down as he lit the cigarette. "The agency is really setting that up?"

Hudson laughed for a long while. A businesswoman at the far end of the room eyed him with annoyance, but he failed to notice her gaze. As his laugh died down, he said, "No, not the agency, some of the team members at New Compass Travel. They heard it was the last day for us. A little tip of the hat for our service."

Donaldson whistled. "Wow, an outside company has to take care of us?"

"Typical government, I'd say," Hudson replied, looking down at his scuffed black boots. He hadn't bothered to polish them since the supervisory staff were let go last month. "Still, I'll miss this place." His eyes moved around the greys and whites of the room. "Can't believe this station use to house over a thousand officers at any one time." His eyes returned to Donaldson. "Well, a thousand humans, that is."

"What is it now, seven?" Donaldson let out a sigh. "Everyone else replaced by a droid. I was mad like we all were at the beginning, but frankly our robot friends have been doing a better job than we ever could."

Hudson gave a satisfied nod, prompting Donaldson to continue, "Tax collection is up, use of force is down—way down. Shots have only been fired a handful of times across all of

Arzonian space, with no misses. Not to mention their drug and human smuggling interception is higher than when it was just our flesh and blood."

"Ya, but how many of those stats are pumped up to keep the Synthetic Officer Induction Program moving full speed ahead and to justify the cost to the public?"

"Maybe." Donaldson shrugged. "If you asked me a few years ago, I probably would have agreed with you, but I bet the person in charge of the stats has been laid off for a while. Now a machine collects them, and I doubt it's making up numbers."

Hudson nodded after a moment, appearing to come around to his friend's way of thinking. "I can't fault them though. Better interview skills, pulse reading, microfacial expression recognition… We can't compete. Plus, they are always pleasant, even when arresting people for absolutely horrendous crimes."

Donaldson chuckled. "Remember all the surly officers when we started? Crusty and jaded."

"Like Melbourne?" Hudson offered with an amused gleam in his eye.

"Yes, exactly like Melbourne. I heard he led the port in complaints."

Hudson waved a hand though the air as he said, "He would have fit in great at a place like Starshore Pass. I heard the morale there was beyond zero."

Donaldson opened his mouth to speak before adjusting his train of thought and saying, "And yet somehow our medium-sized port is the last place to still have human officers."

"Beat Redford Valley by a whole two days," Hudson replied with a thin smile.

"The first and only time we beat the flagship port at something," Donaldson replied, a touch of sadness in his voice. There was a lull in the conversation before he added, "Speaking of time, shouldn't we head back?" His eyes gravitated to the bright sign over the exit to the smoking room.

Hudson shrugged. "Who cares? We're unemployed tomorrow; I don't think anyone is watching." He flicked some ash down the grate underneath them. "The droids aren't going to report it."

"Ain't that the truth. But, you know, I would like to earn the last day of my pay. Build one last memory before the cake and forced retirement."

"The agency sure lucked out with an exception when they hired you. Broke the mold, I guess."

Donaldson nodded, adjusted his defensive vest. "You know, thinking about it, I'm proud of us. Our coworkers, I mean. I'm surprised more officers didn't snap at entitled travellers, considering we knew our time was coming to a grinding halt."

Hudson scratched his thinning hair. "The idea did pop into my head a few times, but I think we're all just too tired. I, for one, am glad to finally have some certainty in my life. The last five years have been grueling. Management holding our jobs over our heads after the union collapsed. At least now we know the droids are one hundred percent of the frontline staff, as of tomorrow."

Donaldson took a final inhale of his cigarette as he said, "Remember the animosity the droids got when the first dozen hit the floor for the trial?"

"I do. Damn, it went by fast. It was the anniversary of my first year on the job when the group of twelve starting working." Hudson laughed. "Remember the reports from Redford? All those officers walking off the job under union 'guidance.' The local at that port was always gung ho."

"And it just made the droids look better in everyone's eyes: the public, the government, management. The union didn't know it, but they put an expiry date on our jobs the moment they did that," Donaldson said as he looked to his wrist device for the third time in under a minute.

"Fine," Hudson said, as he flicked his finished cigarette down the grate, "I can see you eying the exit sign. A few more travellers before we hit the road for good."

Hudson watched as Donaldson began to pivot, prompting him to add, "It's only because you're so insistent. I would stay here for the rest of the shift if it were up to me. Imagine we find something? Like a few kilos of Skillion Red and have to stay overtime on our last day? Who would we even call to authorise it? The president of the agency? Does she even still have a job, or did the droids take that one too?"

"No, the upper echelons of senior management will always have a job, I suppose. I read in the email that Starshore still has a chief at it, and we can call her for anything. She'd probably laugh and let us stay for it. What does she care? She's out on the street tomorrow, just like us. Only directors and tertiary staff will make up the human element."

Hudson shook his head in frustration as they left their spot and headed for the large glass doors at the other side of the room. The two officers walked past several security walls that scanned their faces and clearance cards before granting them entry through the employee entrance at the far end of the arrivals level.

They entered the baggage hall and waved at an officer who was headed towards the immigration quadrant. The aging officer hardly acknowledged the two, but the column of droids that followed him waved back in unison, their grey faces lighting up at the prospect of being recognised by their colleagues.

As they marched off in unison, Hudson admired their slick blue paint jobs and the simulated patch on their shoulder. "They always wave," he said, after a moment. "And our former colleagues couldn't understand why the public liked the robots better. Always smiling; always happy."

"Such a mystery," Donaldson replied, before gesturing with his chin at the surly officer who rode the escalator. "Not like Heartford. Why didn't he quit a few years back like the bulk of them?"

The two walked past a group of impatient travellers who

stood by an empty luggage belt as Hudson replied, "I asked him that and he said he had never quit anything before, and he wasn't going to start at sixty-two." He turned his attention to Donaldson. "Why didn't you? I mean, for me it didn't make sense financially, but why not you?"

Donaldson shrugged. "I guess Heartford and I have more in common than I like to think. But I don't know. I would rather say I stuck it out and only left my post when I was relieved."

"That's pretty noble," Hudson said with a sideways glance.

"I'm serious. Plus, like you, I have another job lined up. But I'll take a few months off first; see more of the Queendom. I never travelled when I was younger, always moving on to the next goal."

"The next stage of life…" Hudson trailed off before adding, "Been there."

They entered the secondary inspection hall and Donaldson's eyes scanned the forty-two robotic faces that each stood behind a counter, performing baggage examination and conducting interviews. The two human officers took adjacent counters beside one another at the far side of the hall. Donaldson flicked his light to green and the service droid at the front of the snaking line gestured for the next traveller to head in Donaldson's direction.

The officer watched as a lone male traveller dressed in the finest New Terran Empire-styled suit sauntered over and sized up Donaldson before throwing his suitcase up on the counter. The man folded his arms and, with his voice oozing venom, said, "Of course, I get the human."

"Declaration chip, please," Donaldson said, ignoring the comment.

The man shook his head before pushing out a closed fist and turning his wrist-mounted device towards the officer. Donaldson scanned the device and waited for the contents of the application to download to his terminal.

The traveller narrowed his eyes as Donaldson continued to ignore him, adding, "I'm glad you guys are out of a job. You've had it too good for too long. I'll gladly pay more crowns in tax if it ensures the robots stay and I don't have to see you anymore."

"You know, for all your love of the robots, it was one that referred you in here," Donaldson said with an amused expression.

"Just get this over with—I have places to be." The man's voice continued to get louder with each word he uttered.

Hearing this, two synthetic officers approached from nearby counters. "Excuse me, officer. I have detected tense body language and a raised voice pitch from the subject you are in the process of interviewing. Do you require assistance?" the droid on the right asked.

Donaldson looked to the speaking robot and replied, "I'm fine for now, thank you."

The man interjected again, "Yes, droids, I want assistance. I want you to serve me, not this vintage … fossil."

Donaldson raised an eyebrow at the odd insult before moving his face closer to the man and saying, "You know, you're awfully cavalier for someone who's dealing with a man who will be unemployed in mere minutes, regardless of how I act."

The man scoffed and sputtered, "Are you threatening me?" He looked to the synthetic officers and pointed at Donaldson. "You hear that, headlights? H-he *threatened* me. Uttering threats is a crime—arrest him!"

The droids simulated a blink in tandem before the lead one spoke again, "Officer Donaldson merely pointed out a fact just now. I have run four hundred and sixty-two simulations and do not detect any threat being uttered by Officer Donaldson. Good day, sir." Both robots pivoted and moved to their counters, immediately switching their overhead lights to green.

Donaldson smiled a big toothy grin at the man, before asking him several questions about his trip to the outer rim of the New Terran Empire. Unsurprisingly, the man replied only with single word responses.

Donaldson opened the hard-shelled suitcase and removed a

pair of folded trousers. His lips curled in amusement, as he spotted the corks of six bottles of alcohol rolled up in shirts. He blinked twice before looking up at the traveller.

The man pointed at the bottles, his voice defensive as he claimed, "I declared those."

Donaldson turned his head and looked at his terminal read-out. "Oh sir, we both know that isn't the truth."

The man went to open his mouth to speak when Donaldson continued, "Normally I'm pretty lenient when it comes to alcoholic beverages. *Usually* I give two or three bottles on top of your exemption, then charge on the rest." He pointed a calm finger at the droids working farther away. "But they don't. They perform their job to the letter of the law. And when it comes to duty and tax rates, they make you pay right up to the decimal place, no rounding down." Donaldson was grinning now. "Since you wanted the robots to help you before, who am I to stand in the way of that? Your wish is granted."

Donaldson looked to the droid who had spoken to the traveller prior and said, "Officer S.K. Nine, I require assistance."

The droid raised its head before switching the counter light to red. It moved at a quickened pace from around the counter and took position beside Donaldson before saying, "How may I be of assistance?"

"Please do up a forced payment for six undeclared bottles of alcohol." Donaldson looked to his terminal once more to confirm what he had read prior, before adding, "Mr. Stewart here declared no alcohol at all on his declaration chip, so no exemption is to be given today."

The droid blinked once before gingerly removing the bottles from the suitcase and scanning them.

The man uncrossed his arms and sputtered, "No, wait! It's a mistake. The robot upstairs was faulty; I told it what I had. The chip... I typed it in. I must have pressed the wrong button."

"How could you have pressed the wrong button if the droid was faulty? Which is it?" Donaldson asked. While any onlooker would see that his face was stern, he was quite enjoying the poetic justice occurring before him.

The droid ceased scanning the last bottle and looked at Donaldson. "Officer, upon completing my scan, I have determined these bottles to be correctly assessed as alcohol. No discrepancies detected to indicate they house narcotics." Donaldson nodded, prompting the droid to turn its gaze to the traveller. "Please scan your wallet or credit application on the reader at the front of the counter. Your total is displayed there."

"Damn he's fast, huh?" Donaldson said, and gestured to the flashing orange payment terminal to his right.

"I refuse! I want an appeal."

Donaldson went to speak, but thought better of it. The lull in the conversation was filled by S.K. Nine, who said, "Appeals only occur as a result of seizure action. There is no appeal as a result of a forced payment."

"Then I refuse to pay."

S.K. Nine opened his mouth to speak, but Donaldson put a hand out and said, "No interstellar travel until all outstanding fees, fines, or taxes owing have been paid. Oh, and you wouldn't be getting your alcohol back. I hope you don't have business outside the Queendom, because you aren't getting to it."

The man looked to S.K. Nine, which responded by saying, "Officer Donaldson is correct in his statement."

"You law enforcement types are all the same—always have each other's back, never the people's!" the man proclaimed, waving a trembling hand about himself. "It says service on your stupid patch, and I didn't get any service today." He ground his teeth before mumbling something incoherent and moved over to the payment terminal. As he scanned his device against the screen, he added, "This is ridiculous. Can I go now? You've already torn my stuff apart."

"Certainly," Donaldson said, looking at his holoscreen to see the payment was accepted. He looked at the empty suitcase and nodded, satisfied there were no hidden compartments.

The man hastily packed up his things and departed, his face red with anger.

As the man headed for the exit doors, Hudson moved from his counter and over to Donaldson. He looked down at his watch and said, "That's your last traveller as an officer. We are out of a job in six minutes."

Donaldson smiled. "Plenty of time for one more."

Hudson laughed. "Come on, be a typical government employee for once in your life. Let's get that cake. The robots clearly don't need us."

S.K. Nine turned and looked at the two officers. "I had not been informed that it was your last shift with the agency." It extended a plastisteel hand and added, "Thank you, gentlemen, for your service. It has been a pleasure to work with you."

Both Donaldson and Hudson shook its outstretched hand and offered thanks to their replacement. A moment passed before S.K. Nine returned to its original counter and switched the overhead light to green. A family of six quickly approached, each member looking more annoyed than the last.

"I'll miss this place," Donaldson said as they began to depart the secondary hall.

"I bet you won't miss guys like that," Hudson countered, throwing a thumb behind him in the direction of the exit doors. "I heard how he spoke to you."

Donaldson adjusted his duty belt as he replied, "Oh, I don't know. Guys like that build memories, not to mention character. Thick skin, too. All good qualities."

Hudson laughed as he scanned his ID badge on a security door that led down to the lower levels of the station. As they moved through the dreary hallway, he added, "So you made him pay on his booze?"

"Yup. The Queendom is safe now," Donaldson said, prompting both officers to laugh.

"Would have been more interesting if it was drugs, or a bag full of guns," Hudson said, appearing to look back into his familiar memory vault as he added, "Remember the old days before the nanoscans? A bag full of beam rifle parts wasn't all that rare."

"Wasn't all that common either," Donaldson replied, as they stepped around an automated cart full of containers. "But in all honesty, it was the little things that made the job worthwhile. Sure, drugs and guns get the most attention, but other than a pile of paperwork, there isn't much to do. You seize them, arrest the person, and then intel comes and picks it up. But immigration cases, cracking someone who's been lying for hours, or in this case making an entitled person pay for their booze… It's that sort of thing that got me up in the mornings."

"You and I are two very different people," Hudson replied.

"You would think that in seventeen years of knowing each other, you would have come to realise that."

They both laughed as they turned down a short hallway. Donaldson knocked on a frosted glass door labelled, "NEW COMPASS TRAVEL."

The door swung open a moment later, where a woman in a party hat stood. Upon seeing the two officers she said, "You made it!"

"We wouldn't miss cake for anything," Hudson said with a grin.

"Well, we got plenty of it," she said. "Two of your colleagues have already been here for almost an hour."

They entered the office where a small party awaited them to wish them a happy retirement. The woman handed both Donaldson and Hudson a small cup of beer.

Donaldson raised the cup above his head in a toast and said, "To entitled travellers, a happy retirement, and our synthetic replacements."

A small cheer came from the party guests before everyone took a sip of their drinks. The sounds of casual banter soon followed.

# "REMEMBER US IN YOUR SONGS"

The battalions of men stood in tight formations upon the dry plains. Their banners fluttered in the warm breeze as a group of officers stood upon the shaded ridge behind them. General Salvner's steed whinnied and repositioned its hooves on the crusted dirt as the sound of war drums thundered in the distance. The orc hoards were upon them.

"Judging by the racket, I would say they are moving to make contact with us from the west," Captain Hammond said from Salvner's right, atop a horse of his own. He raised his hand to his forehead to wipe the thick layer of sweat that covered his brow.

The troops below shifted their weight as the sounds of the orc advance echoed off the trunks of the distant trees that lay just before the horizon.

"The scouts were indeed correct, it seems," Salvner replied as he patted his horse on the neck, for it continued to show signs of anxiety at the approaching drums.

"Do you think the report on their numbers was accurate as well, my lord?" Hammond asked, as the marching calls of the orcs became audible as they drew nearer.

"Twenty thousand? I fear that is much too low," Salvner

replied, as he took his eyes from the horizon for a moment. "If Ire'ram is still the commander of his lands, he should be able to summon much more to his cause."

"Our runners did report that border disputes have kept him busy since the start of the season. Might have taken up a large portion of his army," Hammond responded. "But if the prophecy has fallen out of favour with the orcs just like it did our kings, well…"

The war drums reached their climax, and the banners of the orc monarchies flew high above their battalions as they exited the treeline in the distance. Three riders emerged from the centre formation, the black and silver of their armors gleaming in the sun.

Salvner smirked at the sight. "It is always a good day when orcs fight by our side."

The riders moved up the escarpment and passed through Salvner's personal guard. The largest of the orcs came closest. He removed the cumbersome wide-brimmed helmet and let his oily black hair fall against his shoulders.

"General Salvner," he said, in a guttural attempt at the common tongue. "My regrets that we could not ride here faster, but I bring news."

Salvner tightened his grip on his horse's reins. He knew the nature of the news before it was spoken, for orcs only ever carried bad news. "Come now, Ire'ram, worse news than our world on the brink of death?"

The orc prince lowered his head, clicking his jagged teeth together once before saying, "The lowborn elves march on us as well. My rear guard held them at bay, but those three thousand were nothing compared to their numbers." He paused, his split tongue working double duty to achieve the proper pronunciation of the common language. "My estimate is no less than fifty thousand and their forward echelon has elementals in their ranks."

"Elementals?" Hammond questioned. "Those separatists haven't been honoured by the elves in hundreds of years."

"It is true," the orc to the right of Ire'ram spoke up. "I saw them with my own eyes." The orc's face hardened. "Or are you calling me a liar?" He began to dismount his horse, a hand wrapped around the hilt of a dagger that was tucked into his boot.

Ire'ram put his hand out and kept the lieutenant in his saddle. He first spoke in the flowing orc cadence, but switched his language after several syllables. "I'm sure the man meant no offence and is not questioning your honour, Kal'ti. He is just as taken aback as you are by such a proposition."

The orc named Kal'ti adjusted his back as he snarled at Hammond.

Salvner noticed the elaborate wolf and axe house sigil emblazoned on the lieutenant's saddle. "I fought with your father," he said, attempting to diffuse the situation.

Kal'ti looked to the general, his cat-like yellow eyes sizing the man up. "What battles?" he asked. While his tone was aggressive, Salvner recognised orc curiosity was usually carried in such a way.

"Malister River was the most recent, but that's getting up there now," Salvner replied, a bead of sweat entering his eye. The heat was starting to swell as the sun reached its central spot in the midday sky.

"My father speaks highly of that battle," Kal'ti replied. "Told me the man armies fought valiantly. Told me that he split many a lowborn in half."

"Of that I have no doubt," Salvner said, with a fist pressed against his chest plate.

"General," Ire'ram said, his horse clapping its hooves with impatience. "What is your thought on the elf units? The use of elementals concerns you, no?"

"Certainly," Salvner replied. "But my men are ready. I knew that others would interpret the prophecy as we had, but if I'm being truthful, I thought we would have had more time, and our defenses already mustered in the new world before they arrived. It appears it is not to be."

"I never thought they would decode it at all," Ire'ram said. "Elves have always scoffed at ideas of man—and ideas of orc, for that matter."

"Too busy sipping their wines," Kal'ti said under his breath. "Very full of themselves for such half-breed runts."

"They seem to have liked our ideas about catapults well enough," Hammond replied, chuckling to himself.

Kal'ti shrugged, his chainmail jangling as he did so. "They recognised talent for once."

"I assume the elves will come from the north of us?" Salvner asked, ignoring the side banter between the junior officers.

"If I had to guess, I would venture that," the orc prince replied, looking over his shoulder to the tree line where his formations stood, awaiting orders.

"Move your troops to cover our eastern flank. We will fight the pointy-eared barbarians when they come. You've lost enough troops just getting here, Ire'ram."

The orc prince placed his fist over his double heart. "The race of men has always been gracious, but know that we orcs are ready for more lowborn blood."

"My lord prince," Hammond said, "did you see any allies of the elves marching with them?"

"No," Ire'ram said. "The elves march alone." He bowed in his saddle towards General Salvner before turning his horse around and riding away down the ridge, his officers riding at his flanks.

Hammond scoffed. "The elves could never keep an alliance for very long, could they?"

Salvner let out a sigh, for he was tired of his subordinates always underestimating their greatest adversary. "They have enough sense to bring the excommunicated back into their fold after three hundred years; they are taking this prophecy seriously, it seems."

He looked over his shoulder and commanded a nearby lieutenant, "Tristian, alert the officers below. Tell them the orcs will cover our flank to the east and to expect elf legions shortly."

Hammond stirred on his horse, circling it about once. "You know this prophecy could sure hurry up and come to pass."

*"Only after fifty days of perpetual rain will the sun emerge and bring with it a ceaseless heat. The light will shine though the pebbles of the conquered land and the realm will gleam behind the opening,"* Salvner quoted the forbidden text. He tapped his saddle pack to ensure the book he valued so highly was still tucked away safely. "It will open when it's good and ready."

He looked over his shoulder to the arched boulders in the distance. The way those rocks had been stacked, clinging together to defy gravity, was an impossible feat for men or elf alike. They were even too unwieldy for the largest of trolls of the first succession to lift before they became stunted and wild at the dawn of the second.

Salvner watched as the orc formations moved in front of his own, the officers bowing to their counterparts as a sign of appreciation for their alliance. By the time the orcs had amalgamated into their groups again, the sun's heat was becoming unbearable.

The portal opened then.

A shining visage of rippling pink, vibrant purples, and an orange the colour of dawn. The orcs observed it first, their calm demeanor standing in contrast to the rear guard of men, who scrambled over each other to bear witness to the awe of such a thing.

Salvner nodded in self-fulfillment and any sense of doubt he had been feeling melted away. While he had bet his life on this prophecy, he was glad to finally be vindicated as correct. "Send word to the convoy; tell them to begin entering the rift," he said to a nearby officer.

As the officer moved off to a sound of hooves, Salvner

watched as Ire'ram rode up the ridge towards him. "It is a wonderous sight, general," the orc prince said, upon reaching Salvner's side.

"I've commanded my unarmed to begin moving. Have you as well, your highness?"

Ire'ram shook his head. "To ensure your orc brothers could answer your call, we left earlier than our own non-combatants. They are still a half day behind us."

Salvner cocked his head and placed a hand over his chest plate. "You should have spoke sooner, Ire'ram. Please let me task a formation to find your people and guide them here. There are untamed bands that still roam this province. I could not sleep in the new world, knowing your innocents were attacked."

Ire'ram bowed in his saddle. "Worry not; my non-combatants march with two legions of my best border guards. They are in good hands. My wife rides with them, and she is frightened by no lowborn elf."

A disturbance of the branches in the distance prompted Salvner to look north. A flock of birds disembarked from their perch in hurried flight. A silent marching formation of gold and white moved from the foliage.

"Ah, the menace make their appearance," Salvner said, gesturing with a gloved hand as the sun caught the intricacies of their armor.

"Good. My ranks will be pleased to avenge the three thousand lost this morning," Ire'ram said, turning back to face the general. "Shall I tell my officers to make contact with the enemy and buy more time for your non-combatants to move thought the rift? I can tell how restless my soldiers are getting."

Salvner could see in his peripherals how still the orc formations stood. *If this is them unruly, I wonder how they look when they are at full battle discipline*, he thought.

He turned his head and watched as a thin trickle of civilians moved from the trees behind his position and towards the shimmering archway of light. He chewed his tongue with annoyance as they were taking longer than he had hoped.

Salvner looked to the orc prince. "No, hold fast, your highness. Our cavalry will make short work of them. But have your archers move into range, if you please."

Ire'ram smirked. "My archers need the practice." He moved over to the edge of the ridge and whistled before pulling a red flag from his saddle. He held it up and let the wind gather on the fabric. The sound of bootsteps thundered up from below as the orc troops moved into their ordered positions.

There was a lull as the elf army stood at the edge of the tree-line and Ire'ram's troops reached their ordered stop. A silence engulfed the plains, and Salvner recognised it for what it was. The kind of silence that only occurs at the certainty of a battle about to commence.

The silence was broken as the forward brigade of elf troops began to march forth. Salvner scanned the advancing forces and estimated it at five thousand strong.

"They'll be ready for arrows, but not the horses," Salvner said to Hammond, who rode up alongside him. "Signal our cavalry to commence the charge."

He knew his orders would be delayed in reaching the captain of the mounted troops, but the general was counting on this. By the time the horses charged forth, the elves would be in the perfect kill zone.

Hammond passed Salvner's command to another officer before returning to his position beside the general. "They are overconfident; they don't suspect a thing," Hammond said in a boastful tone.

Ire'ram moved from his perch on the ridge and over to Salvner, saying, "My archers are ready. Once your cavalry breaks their line, our arrows will finish them off."

Salvner did not reply, growing increasingly concerned by how quickly the elf formation was moving. His eyes gravitated to the remaining forty-five thousand elves that began to advance, but at a slower and more deliberate pace. The general looked down at his formation of troops. The officers stood with their backs to the enemy, eyes gazing up to him as they awaited the order to engage. Salvner ignored their stares, as he held out hope the cavalry would arrive in time.

He watched the advancing force and became aware of just how many seasons it had been since he had squared off against a proper elf army.

The sound of thundering hooves racing from the eastern tree-line caused Salvner to forget the thought. A full formation of horse-mounted troops roared out of the shady trees and moved towards the unsuspecting elf units in the distance. Swords and lances gleamed in the sun and the snarling of horses could be heard moving across the plains.

The forward elf formation stopped its march, and Salvner could imagine the whites of their eyes widening at such a horrific sight—no doubt a scramble of chaos erupting through their ranks. Salvner smiled as he could see the eastern flank of the elf's forward line begin to retreat in on itself.

Hammond cackled as he said, "Nothing like cavalry to give even the mightiest of warriors pause."

"No discipline at the sight of horse lords," Ire'ram said with a quick nod.

Salvner's grin vanished as quickly as it had formed, for it was his eyes that were now wide. While hundreds of elves had begun to disperse, the centre of the formation remained in place. Their armor was different from those that surrounded them. The pikes they carried were on display now that their taller comrades no longer shrouded their existence.

"Dwarves…" he began to say, but the word was lost to the wind.

The dwarves turned their pikes eastward in one synchro-nised step, in preparation for the cavalry charge.

"They played us for fools," Hammond said as he sat forward in his saddle.

There was nothing that could be done. The cavalry was committed; it would be up to their lead riders to recognise the threat and turn away. With almost no time to maneuver, the odds were not in the favour of men.

Salvner could see the wave of horses halt as they refused to run into the sharpened pikes. Soldiers were flung from their saddles and quickly trampled under foot and hoof alike. The dwarves quickly advanced and thrust the steel into the hesitant beasts.

The surviving cavalry officers whirled their steeds northward in an attempt to circle back for the safety of the treeline. Salvner could see dozens of mounted troopers being cut down from the rear of the formation as they turned too slowly to exit the reach of the dwarf pikes.

"So much for the elves not maintaining alliances," Salvner said under his breath.

"Captain Saint Laurent saw the threat," Hammond replied. "We will be able to pull back the cavalry and flank the elves from the rear. All is not lost, general."

Salvner was hardly listening as he saw the bulk of the elf legions at the far end of the field shift ranks as well. The cavalry unit was still turning in a vain attempt to escape.

He watched as thousands of arrows shimmered like glass as they entered the air. The surviving riders had inadvertently moved into the archers' range. Salvner could hear the sound of his teeth grinding as the cavalry was torn apart by the volley.

Seeing this, Ire'ram moved to the cliff edge and waved his red flag in three distinct motions. His archers began to loose arrows of their own on the mixed enemy formation.

While the arrows cut down several of the dwarf pikemen, the bulk of the elf units were unfazed as they raised their shields. Salvner watched as only a handful of his once infamous cavalry unit hobbled back into the protection of the treeline. The silver of Captain Saint Laurent's armour was not among the survivors.

Salvner could see the elves were moving forward again. The

orc arrows deflected off their raised shields, while the surviving dwarf units fell back towards the safety of the massive formations in the distance.

"Hammond, order Telford and Simmons forward. Engage them," Salvner said, pointing at the forward units.

Hammond kicked his horse in the ribs as he moved to tell the runners of the general's command.

Several minutes passed and Salvner watched as his formations stood still. He tightened his grip on the reins in anger. The orders were taking too long to get to his officers below. The general saw a runner move up to Captain Telford and another into the second formation to alert Captain Simmons. Both units began to march forward seconds after.

"Ire'ram, cease the volley," Salvner said in as polite a tone as he could muster, the loss of his cavalry unit still stinging his mind.

The orc prince nodded before moving the red flag in a slicing motion. The arrows ceased falling immediately. While Salvner was aware he was moving his units into range of the enemy archers, he knew the elves would not risk the possibility of hitting their own troops.

Telford and Simmons marched their troops forward before breaking into a run when they stood less than fifty metres from the golden formation ahead. Salvner felt a sense of calm move through him. While he had lost the cavalry, he was confident his two best units would make short work of the forward elf line.

Salvner turned his attention to Ire'ram, who had pulled a green flag from his saddle and waved it above his head. He was gesturing north to the bulk of the enemy troops. Before the general could inquire which order the orc prince had given, his attention turned back to the plains below.

A hundred unshielded elf troops sprinted from the rear of the battlefield. From such a great distance, it was hard to see the particulars of these units, but the speed at which they charged told the general they were unarmored.

A STONE'S THROW AWAY FROM PARADISE

*Runners,* Salvner began to think, but ceased the thought as he contemplated that there would be no reason to send out so many messengers into a single formation. The new arrivals amalgamated into the formation quickly enough and disappeared into the mix of gold and silvers of the clashing troops.

Hammond rode up beside Salvner a moment later. "My lord, Captain Richards is requesting his troops move forward and engage."

"Richards can wait," Salvner replied, not breaking eye contact with the battle below.

"My lord, he was quite insistent," Hammond added. He hesitated before continuing, "He mentioned Hartous Ridge. That you two had an agreement—"

"I said, he can wait!" Salvner hissed, waving his hand to silence Hammond. He did not have time to worry about Richards and his pathetic rivalry with Telford.

A series of brilliant red and vibrant blue flashes erupted from the heart of the battle. Salvner clenched his jaw tight as he witnessed dozens of his troops fly backwards.

"The elementals have joined the fray," Ire'ram said as he moved beside the human officers.

"Pull our troops back," Salvner ordered, turning his attention from the slaughter in the distance.

"Sire?" Hammond asked in disbelief. "Their retreat will leave them open to enemy archers."

"Do as I say!" Salvner commanded. "They're dead if they stay there."

Hammond nodded with a grimace, before riding off to inform the runners of the command.

Salvner turned to look at the portal in the distance. Hundreds of civilians and dozens of wagons moved towards it. The evacuation was picking up speed, but it still was not fast enough.

"How are we to hold them Ire'ram?" Salvner asked as he turned his head towards the orc prince. "The prophecy was unclear as to how long it will remain open. It could last several days. We will not survive the night at this rate."

Ire'ram frowned, replying in the orc dialect before correcting himself, "We will hold them. I have fought elf expansionism my entire life and I have not lost yet." He raised the green flag from his side and waved it. A formation of orcs charged forward. "The elementals lack stamina," Ire'ram added with a grin.

As the orc hoard moved forward, the sky blackened as a volley of arrows raced towards the approaching reinforcements. Salvner recognised this move for what it was: the elf commander showing how much he feared the prospect of Ire'ram's warriors advancing. The orc troopers raised their shields and merged into a phalanx formation.

Salvner watched at his runners navigated the chaos and successfully found Captains Telford and Simmons. The human forces began to retreat soon after. The elf archers were still occupied with the orc horde and failed to adjust their aim as the human brigade broke contact and began to withdraw westward.

Ire'ram waved his red flag, and the orc archers began to hammer the exhausted elf formation. The arrows ceased after a volley as the orc units made contact with the enemy.

Salvner turned his attention from the dwindling flashes of the elementals' weapons, as he detected movement in the treeline to the west. His heart stopped as he looked past his retreating force.

Trolls. Two dozen of them, clad in full battle armor, lurched from the darkness of the woods.

"Shift arrows!" Salvner yelled to Ire'ram and pointed at the advancing monstrosities.

The yellows in Ire'ram's eyes widened at the sight. Never in the annals of recorded history had an alliance existed between elves and trolls.

The towering behemoths swung their axes across the helpless human force. Salvner froze, unable to process the amount of carnage that was occurring before his eyes.

"My lord," Hammond said. He sounded out of breath. "My

lord, something has happened." Before Salvner could reply the officer continued, "Sire, the portal… It grows smaller. Look."

Salvner turned, his hands trembling. He looked past the hundreds of civilians and could see the rift had indeed changed. Gone were the purples and pinks, being replaced by a burning yellow. A gap between the stone archway and the swirling light could be seen as it shrank in size.

Salvner shook his head, unable to focus on that right now. He moved to the edge of the cliff, stopping beside Ire'ram. He gestured to Captain Richards, pointing westward as he yelled, "Engage the trolls!"

Ire'ram lowered his red flag as his archers got to work on the new threat, before pulling the green flag from his saddle. He waved it in a cross-like motion, which prompted a battalion to fall in behind the human troops.

Salvner was appreciative of the assistance, but he could not help but feel like they were committing too many troops to this new force and not enough on the massive elf army that stood in the distance.

Salvner watched the trolls continue to slaughter the remainder of his retreating force as Captain Richards and the orcs charged towards them. His mind span, trying to calculate the elf commander's next move. Combine the chaos of battle with the closing portal and it was almost too much for him to handle. His eyes darted between the two skirmishes of trolls to the west and elf forces to the north. The glimmer of gold in the distance caught his eyes as the entirety of the elf formation, forty-five thousand strong, resumed their march forward.

Salvner did not hesitate. "Hammond, get our archers to focus on the advancing elf troops."

"Y-yes, sire," Hammond replied, knowing the human archers lacked the range or stamina of the orcs. Their offensive output would be minimal at best, but at least it would slow down the advancing force.

Before Hammond rode away, Salvner added, "Tell all our

troops except Lawson to begin falling back to the rift. Have her engage the forward elf formation and assist our orc brethren."

Ire'ram looked over his shoulder, overhearing the command. No doubt he felt his orcs were more than up to the task, but he was not going to refuse the help. Not as flashes of elemental weapons continued in the distance.

Salvner heard the thunder of hooves fade off behind him as the officers hurried to inform the troops below of the retreat order.

Captain Lawson looked up towards the escarpment, her eyes locking on Salvner's thin face. She raised her sword to her shoulder before extending it in the salute for those who were about to die, and led her battalion forward.

Salvner closed his eyes for a moment as she had clearly seen through his order. The officer knew she would not be seeing the new world, but she was a warrior through and through, like her father and grandfather before her.

Salvner pulled on the reins of his horse and moved down the ridge to join his forces that raced in the direction of the rift. As he reached the plains, he ordered his steed to stop and watched as hundreds of civilians vanished into the rift. Several wagons followed suit, with many more on the way.

Ire'ram rode up beside him. "Excellent strategy, general. We will force them into this chokepoint here," he said, gesturing to where the ridge and the trees created a natural bottleneck.

Salvner did not reply. Instead, he turned his attention to the hordes of infantry that moved past him, taking position a hundred metres in front of the portal. The orc forces were retreating as well, but at a much slower pace. Salvner contemplated the reason for the hesitation in their ranks and thought, *Perhaps they wonder why they were being held back when a fight with their lowborn rivals is imminent?*

Salvner turned around to face the battlefield as a junior officer yelled, "Trolls!"

Five of the beasts lumbered towards the forward human and

orc force. Lawson's troops began to dwindle as the mammoth-sized axes sliced across her ranks. Salvner felt a moment of sorrow, knowing that Richards had failed to stop the troll advance.

"Pull back the archers," Salvner yelled, looking every which way for Hammond. "Tell them to get back behind our force." He knew moving the archers back would take them out of range of the advancing elf formations, but the trolls were getting dangerously close.

Hearing this exchange between the humans, Ire'ram roared something in his native tongue. Kal'ti bowed before promptly riding off in the direction of the orc archers. Salvner watched as the lieutenant selected two dozen of his archers to break off from the main unit and move towards the trolls. While the brutes were armored to defend against arrows from the sky, they were not equipped to take a volley at chest level, especially not one fired by the strength of an orc.

Salvner gestured to Ire'ram that he was moving back before beginning his ride towards the still shrinking rift. "Back! Closer to the portal," he yelled as he neared the stunned faces of his troops.

The troops did as they were commanded and retreated into the dried stream fifty metres from the rift. The non-combatants had become a trickle now, and Salvner hoped it was because most had ventured into the new world and had not fallen victim to possible elf raiding parties that had flanked their position.

Salvner looked forward. The orc troops remained firm at the first rally point. Prince Ire'ram looked at the shrinking portal before turning back towards the losing battle. The trolls had fallen, but the forty-five thousand elves had reached their forward ranks. Dozens of light flashes signalled a new wave of elementals joining their weary comrades.

"Ire'ram!" Salvner shouted. "Move your forces back."

As he spoke, he could see the armor of dwarf pikemen

moving through the treeline to the east, no doubt having finished off the remnants of the battered cavalry unit.

Salvner looked back and could see the portal was now a fraction of its original size. The yellow border gave way to an underworld red. The non-combatants were all through now.

"Retreat!" Salvner yelled to his troops. "All of you, into the rift."

His units obeyed and began to sprint towards the narrowing opening. Any sense of military order abandoned them the moment the command escaped his lips.

Despite the chaos, the orcs stood their ground, backs to the portal.

"The rift is almost gone!" Salvner shouted, his eyes returning to the orc prince. "Ire'ram, come on."

Ire'ram took a deep breath, his shoulders rising and falling. He adjusted his grip on the reins of his horse and turned around to face Salvner. "Our non-combatants will never make it here," he said, the tone of defeat clinging to his words. His eyes left Salvner's weathered face and he looked back at the advancing elf and dwarf formations. "Without our women, we will die out in the new world as nothing but a whimper."

"No, we can do this together. Fall back with us!" Salvner called out.

The elf forces were almost on them. Their archers could be seen moving to higher vantage points along the ridge line above.

"Never forget that it was the orcs that rode to your aid, even when your own alliance of men failed to believe you," Ire'ram said, unsheathing his sword.

The orc prince turned and roared in his native tongue. His troops echoed his sentiment and began to move forward to meet the enemy forces that approached.

Ire'ram looked over his shoulder and said, "Remember us in your songs."

With that, Ire'ram, the last prince of the House of O'llyn, rode off to join his troops.

Salvner had no choice now. The orcs had made their decision and already their swords crossed with that of the elf menace.

He kicked his horse in the ribs and rode towards the collapsing rift. "Faster! Faster!" he yelled, both to the steed and the few remaining troops who brought up the rear. He felt his horse lose balance on the dried rocks of the stream, but it managed to stay upright and bounded towards the ever-shrinking portal.

In a single moment, Salvner went from being in a scorching valley surrounded by death to a frozen tundra. As his stallion skidded to a halt, he saw the thousands of survivors huddled around the horses and wagons, attempting to keep warm. It was then he felt the bite of the air at his exposed skin, and the sweat under his armor chilled him to the bone.

Salvner looked over his shoulder and saw the swirling expanse was nothing more than a pinprick of light now. A few soldiers tumbled through after him, swearing as their faces met snow.

Then, within the blink of an eye, the light was gone and any connection to their world of old went with it.

Salvner felt his heart drop at the finality of such a thing. At the sacrifice Ire'ram and the orcs had made for them. Depriving themselves of this new world and their chance to live on to ensure the humans could escape.

Salvner looked ahead and saw that several hundred of his people were moving towards the perceived shelter of a group of mountains that jutted over them, just a short ride away.

As Salvner moved past several wagons, Hammond rode up beside him. "This is our new home?" the junior officer asked, as he patted his shivering horse in a vain attempt to free it from the burning cold. "I was expecting more."

"It will be," Salvner replied. "We just have to find our way."

They rode onward and joined the forward group of wandering soldiers.

As the band neared the base of the mountain range, a slight

flicker of light could be see emerging from the mouth of a cave. The troops grinned at the siren-like call and picked up the pace.

Salvner narrowed his eyes as he dismantled his horse, handing the reins to a shivering aid. "Who made the fire?" he whispered to himself as he jogged after the sprinting men.

The group of warriors and peasants stopped dead in their tracks ahead of him. As Salvner caught up to them, he pushed through the crowd and quickly understood why they had ceased their charge in the pursuit of warmth.

Standing in the shadows of the fire were six figures. Salvner pulled his blade from its sheath, as the unknown entities were cause for alarm. One of these figures moved from the darkness and Salvner was taken aback by the appearance of it.

Greasy, matted black hair hung down past its face, and a beard was tucked into the furs it adorned. The gap in the furs revealed that its ribcage widened out over its stomach.

While this being walked like a man, its shoulders were broader and hips much more pronounced. Salvner had seen cave dwellers before, but this creature looked like some sort of half-breed ape.

Another abomination crept from the shadows, its beady black eyes watching as dozens of newcomers approached the fire. Gasps and whispers sounded off around the cave as the humans locked eyes on these hideous beings.

One of the ape-men growled, prompting the one closest to pull a sharpened rock out from under its furs. Another emitted a gurgling sound as it produced a crude spear from the shadows.

The largest of the ape-men then came forward. A murderous rage was in its eyes as it lunged towards the invaders who came for its fire. The bright reflections from their armor seemed to send it into a frenzy.

The abomination attempted to batter Salvner's skull in with a sharpened rock, but the veteran anticipated the blow and stepped out of the way, burrowing his sword up into the ape-man's exposed armpit.

The remaining creatures howled and stamped their feet as their comrade collapsed to the ground with a screech. Red blood seeped out of the wound and onto the rocks of the cave floor.

The remaining five half-breeds lunged then. A mix of spears, rocks, and a crude axe moved towards the superior force of men.

In a single flash of steel, all of the half-breeds joined their fallen brother. The humans paid them little mind as they stepped over the bodies to get closer to the fire.

Hammond rolled one of the savages over with his boot and asked, "Sire, what do you think they are?"

"Some sort of local," Salvner said, wiping the blood from his sword with a cloth he pulled from inside his chest plate.

Hammond sucked on his teeth. "As aggressive as an elf and twice as stupid, it seems." He sized up the corpse, seeming to focus on the brow line of their bulbous skulls. "Did they even try to communicate?"

Salvner shook his head. "No. There was no reasoning with them." He paused, slipping his gloves from his scarred hands, and warming them near the fire. "I'll make it a standing order to kill these things on sight."

The sounds of the human survivors moving into the warmth of the cave flooded through the network of tunnels that lay ahead. Salvner would appoint sentries to venture deeper into the mountains—but later, after the cold had left their bones. He anticipated minimal losses as these creatures offered little in the way of sport.

# AND TO DUST YOU SHALL RETURN

I knew my mouth was agape, but I cared little for something so trivial. Not when I was gazing upon something so profound. We had finally done it. We had found the edge of space. My brain struggled to put into cohesive thoughts how magnificent it was.

I looked to my co-pilot and let out a shriek of a laugh. "One hundred and seven jumps," I said, my voice shaking with excitement, as I tapped the reader beside my terminal. "One hundred and seven!"

Tyson looked to me, his eyes a little mad, clearly watching the horizon in his peripheral. "It's not what I thought it would be," he said. While my voice radiated excitement, his held a tense aura that slithered between the utterance of every word.

"It makes perfect sense," I said, and unbuckled my flight harness to lean forward. "Of course, the end would look like that." I pointed to the white void several million kilometres ahead. "The opposite of darkness is, of course, light!" That last word had such gravitas to me as it moved across my tongue and out my jittering lips.

Tyson swallowed. "It's not what I thought."

"What did you think then? We would hit a wall of pure energy? Maybe become surrounded by impassible black holes?

A great beast would be lurking around to devour us like those tales the sailors told each other when the seas were seven and the water ran off the edge of the world?"

"I never said those things!" Tyson snapped. "I just thought it would go on forever."

I ignored his comment and clapped my hands together. "Can you believe it; the bonus pay for achieving our goals? For actually getting here, to the end of space." I paused. my heart was beating so hard, it made it hard to concentrate. "We are the first two to ever see it, in all of human history. Hell, even larger than that. In all of history itself." I slapped my forehead in a dumbfounded trance to ensure it was real. "Just beautiful," I said, marvelling at the static brightness of the white void.

As I buckled myself in and grabbed the controls, Tyson's hand lurched forward and seized the steering mechanism. "What are you doing?" he asked, his eyes wild.

"Going in for a closer look. That's what we're here for. That's why we've given up all these years of our lives."

"Shouldn't we look around here before we go straight in?" His voice had lost its edge, but was still somehow dangerous.

"Look around?" I said, a quizzical look on my face. "There's nothing here. We've been in dark space for the last sixty jumps. It has all been the same. Nothing. Nada. Just unending darkness." I looked to the forward viewscreen. "It's just us out here."

Tyson clutched at his harness. "Don't say that."

"Don't say what? That we're all alone—"

"Yes!" Tyson snapped. "Don't say it. I hate it." He closed his eyes and rocked in his chair. "I-I don't like thinking about being so far away from… From…"

He trailed off again, but I understood his sentiment. No rational person wants to realise they are an imperceptible distance away from everything they have ever known. Everything they have ever loved.

I tightened my hands on the controls. "It's our mission, Ty," I said with a twinge of compassion in my voice. I felt his grip loosen from the controls. As they did, I engaged the engines.

"Do a scan," Tyson pleaded, his eyes bolting open as he sensed the ship gaining speed. "Do a scan, please!"

"What's the point? I mean—"

"Do a goddamn scan!" Tyson screamed, causing me to flinch. A thimbleful of adrenaline trickled from my brain.

"All right, all right. Elaam, I'll do it!" I hated to use the philosopher king's name like that, but Tyson had startled me.

I tapped the controls on the side of my armrest and heard the soft pings as our measuring equipment sent out oscillating frequencies in all directions. I drummed my fingers on the side of my chair, knowing no signal would come back.

We sat in relative silence as we waited—the vibrations of our idle engines, the circulation of air, and the constant rhythm of the electronic pings served as our only companions.

After several moments, I broke the silence. "See, there's nothing out there. Now let me drop the buoy so we can report our position."

Tyson snapped his head towards me, his voice on the verge of hysterics. "You haven't dropped it yet?"

"No, I didn't have the time with you telling me to do scans!"

"Drop the buoy! Oh, *expanse*," he cried, using the archaic expression. "No one knows we're here. Oh, expanse—"

"Calm down, I'm doing it," I said, pressing a button on my chair.

I felt a small jolt as the buoy was released. It carried a record of our coordinates and would make the hundred and seven jumps home. I could see Tyson had visibly relaxed, as he too felt the device leave the ship. We sat surrounded by a peculiar silence for several minutes and I truly thought the worst of Tyson's cabin fever-induced paranoia had left him. Then he spoke again, and this time his voice was almost a whisper.

"It's moving."

"What? What was that?" I asked, trying to keep my voice level.

"It's moving. The edge of space, it's moving away from us…" His voice was oddly calm, like his mind was sheltering him from the true meaning of the realisation.

I squinted. "I don't see anything. It looks the same to—"

"Measure the distance point!" he cried. A shaking finger pointed to the white horizon.

I did not wish to argue, so I did as he instructed, but not before I pushed the steering assembly forward. Tyson opened his mouth to speak, but I cut him off by saying, "I'm getting closer to cut down on the delay."

I could not tell if Tyson accepted this answer, but it kept him quiet. The entire time he stared forward, watching the bright expanse creep ever closer to us.

Several minutes passed and I could tell Tyson was getting antsy again. I activated the ion lasers and measured the point where the blackness of our universe ended, and this new realm began. "One decimal five, two, six, three million kilometres," I said, reading the data from my holoscreen. "I don't see any movement," I added, my voice containing a hint of annoyance.

As my words hung in the recycled air around us, for a moment, I thought Tyson had dropped the matter entirely. Just as the thought began to sprout roots in my mind, he said, "Measure it again!" He was really squirming in his seat now.

I gritted my teeth and did as he asked. The beam went out and after a few agonising moments, it came back with the reading of, "One decimal five, two, six, four million kilometres…"

My words dissolved in the air as I said them. He had been right.

The edge was moving from us.

"I knew it!" Tyson exclaimed. "It knew it! Our space is expanding. Or that other … place is shrinking."

I shook my head in disbelief. "Are we seeing the continued

momentum of the big bang? But I-I thought—" I struggled to structure my thoughts into a coherent sentence. "How can— The universe was bright before it happened? The darkness… It doesn't make sense."

"It makes perfect sense!" Tyson replied in a mocking tone as he repeated what I had said before. He leaned forward in his chair. "I was right."

"Let's go investigate, before it gets farther away."

"I don't like this," Tyson said. "I don't like—"

"What are you talking about?" It was my turn to snap at him. "You were one of the first volunteers on the project. You've been to the bottom of the Mariana Trench. Been atop Pluto's peaks. Even did an orbit of Trinity-Nevis' tri-rings in Andromeda. Adventure, exploration, discovery… You said things like that before we even left. Remember?"

"There's discovery, and then there are places no person—no living being—was meant to venture."

"What do you really think we'll find in there? It's open space, nothing else. Bright light as far as the eye can—"

"What's casting the light?" Tyson asked. "What if we go in and the laws of physics as we know them are different—or even worse, don't exist at all? What if we fly apart, fold in on ourselves or—" He cut himself off. His eyes looked as if every ounce of sanity had slipped from them. "What if we find God?"

"Did you take a blow to the head or something?" I asked, grabbing a medical scanner from the overhead storage cabinet on my left. "All the jumps have changed you. You're showing symptoms of Ryker's Syndrome."

"Not the jumps!" he sputtered. "But the years; the sleep-wake, sleep-wake cycles of the cryopods. The distance… I can't wrap my mind around the distance!"

I opened the medical bag and pulled out a scanner. I waved it over Tyson, focusing on his head, and looked at the readings. Unsurprisingly, it showed his heart rate was elevated, but curiously I noted no sign of radiation poisoning. No tumors or signs of cancers. Brainwaves consistent with a stressed individual, but no indicators of any brainstem decay. Everything was within acceptable levels. I returned the scanner to the bag and said, "We won't see a god. Trust me—"

"What's making the light then?"

"It's not light," I replied, but quickly began to backpedal as I struggled to come up with an explanation. "Maybe that is how it looks; we knew if we found the edge of space it would look like something we couldn't even fathom. I don't know why you—"

"If we go in there, we're entering the wrong way." Tyson said, prompting me to stare at him with confusion. "We're looking behind the scenes of the universe; we're not supposed to be there. What if we see it? See behind the curtain of reality itself? See the face of it…"

My cheeks hardened at his psychotic musings. I went to open my mouth, but found myself closing it as I thought, *Where is this God delusion coming from? Before today, he has never mentioned anything like this. He was the one who mocked me for having grand-parents that were part of the Heaven Masses Church.*

"The face of God," Tyson said under his breath, breaking me from my train of thought.

"Are we going in or not?" I asked.

In truth, I'm not sure why I said that when I did, as the question had been rhetorical. I was going in whether he wanted to or not.

"I can only show you my back…" Tyson began to mumble. "What if what we perceive as reality is only its back? What if going in there is to see—"

"If you say the face of God one more time, I—" I felt my fist clench on the steering apparatus. I could not believe a man of science such as Tyson Keating was succumbing to ancient fables and mystical nonsense such as he was.

Tyson sat in silence for a moment before saying, "We should investigate the scans on *this* side of the line. There is something out here; I can feel it. A planet. An asteroid. Some sort of celestial body. Imagine it: the farthest world, the first planet, really. Think of the core samples we could obtain. Something so many years old that we couldn't even comprehend it."

I stayed silent, prompting Tyson to add, "I was right about the expansion; I'm right about the planet. Let's search the scanned data. I'm sure something is out there, on this side of the line."

I took a deep breath, my hand reaching into the medical bag for the rapid dispenser designed to knock out people suffering from fits. "We will go a few thousand kilometres into it and—"

"No! No, please, no!" Tyson begged.

"Let me finish," I added. "We go in and wait for the darkness to catch up to us. We will study the readings and that's all. I'm sure once we're in there, you'll see it will be quite boring."

"A hundred kilometres," Tyson said. "No further."

"No, that's too small. We will barely have moved across the threshold."

"Five hundred, that's it. I mean it."

"A thousand?" I offered, but my voice carried weight behind it.

Tyson did not reply, but I could see him gripping the sides of his flight chair in anticipation for the engines to activate once more.

I pushed the apparatus forward and watched as the white expanse began to grow across the viewscreen. I had to fight myself from speaking then. I wanted to talk to Tyson about the idea of using our jump drives in this new expanse, travelling trillions upon trillions of kilometres in the blink of an eye, but I knew that would push him over the edge and cause him to mutiny. I could see it in his face, and in the way his chest rose and fell in nervous heaves.

*If the man doesn't even want to go a thousand kilometres, then there is no way I can convince him to make a jump inside.*

As we accelerated forward, I had to admit to myself that Tyson's phobias had begun to rub off on me. The idea of being so far away from everything had crept subtly into my psyche, not unlike the way our universe was creeping into the white expanse.

We soon came within the last hundred kilometres of the space we thought of as ours. I could hear Tyson beginning to hyperventilate. As I looked to him, I saw sweat pouring down his face. I truly thought he was going to have a heart attack. It may seem selfish, but in my conquest in the name of scientific curiosity, I kept the steering column forward.

As the brightness of the expanse filled the entire viewscreen, I chewed on my cheek as an unpleasant idea came to the forefront of my mind. I suddenly felt like the last dodo bird looking down the barrel of the sailor's gun as he was about to pull the trigger. Looking extermination right in the eye and not having the cognitive ability to grasp such a concept.

I pulled the throttle back and felt the reactors of the engines behind us begin to vibrate as our speed slowed. Tyson pressed his back into his flight chair, bracing for impact. We grit our teeth as we closed in the gap on the last handful of metres.

Our worry was for naught, as our ship slipped into the white expanse without incident. I felt an enormous weight drift from my shoulders, and I looked over at Tyson. A shocked smile clung to my lips, while he still looked like he had seen a ghost.

"See? No issues," I said as I eyed the instrument panels around me.

Their readings stayed steady, as if nothing had changed. *Because nothing has changed*, I thought with a vague sense of exasperation. *Tyson got into my head for nothing.*

I returned my eyes to the white nothingness ahead and noticed something. The words I had spoken aloud a moment ago had not sounded right. My voice had been different. The echo off the steel around us was dull as well.

Tyson curled his lips before muttering, "Just fly the ship." His voice had a chilling edge to it.

In my mind's eye I thought about the clear serum housed in

the needle that rested in the medical bag beside me. I would not hesitate to use it if I must.

As the we crossed the thousand-kilometre marker, I expected Tyson to speak up, but he never did. He just sat there, his eyes forward on the limitless white. I wanted to turn on the rear-view camera and see the black void creeping along behind us, but I knew seeing that would cause Tyson to lose his grip on the single thread of sanity he had left.

I kept the ship at the same speed for nearly an hour. I feared that by adjusting anything, it would disrupt the fragile equilibrium Tyson and I had unknowingly created between each other. I gulped before slightly increasing the speed. Tyson did not argue at this, either. In fact, I believe he did not notice.

With newfound confidence, I increased the speed even more. This game of pushing the limits of Tyson's patience lasted several million kilometres into the new expanse. It was not until we were travelling at ninety-six percent maximum power of our single engine that Tyson spoke for the first time in hours.

"Slow down…"

I turned to look at him, but his voice became hysterical.

"Slow down! There's something there!" He pointed forward.

I pulled the steering mechanism back towards me, feeling the ship shutter before beginning to drift. I had to squint to see what he was talking about, but I did see it. A black spot in the distance.

"Is that the end of it?" I asked.

I had hardly gotten the words out before Tyson started to yell, "The face of God! The face of God! The face of God!"

It was incessant.

"Tyson, stop. No, it's not." I placed my right arm across his body as he began to unbuckle his harness. I feared for my safety at what he might do. In an attempt to calm him, I added, "I'll zoom in with the cameras. You'll see."

This was indeed the worst thing to say at that moment as Tyson screamed, "No! The face of God—we can't look at it!"

He was strong. He began to rise, despite my arm pinning him down. His eyes were rabid, his mouth foaming with rage and terror. Insanity no longer probed the outcroppings of his mind, but had taken full form.

"The face!" he screamed again.

I had no choice. While still fighting him with one arm, I moved my free hand into the medical bag and retrieved the syringe. In one moment, I was wrestling with him; in the next, the contents of the needle were descending into his neck.

His eyes jerked down at the needle with horror, his hands balling into fists. He swung at me as I pulled the needle from his tissue, but his knuckles did not get very far. His head sagged and I could hear him mumble the words one last time: "The face."

His eye lids went heavy and then he was unconscious in the chair beside me. I tossed the needle over my shoulder and fastened the belt around Tyson's body, tightening it as I did so. It was just me now, left to discover whatever the black spot was that lay ahead against the horizon of white.

I typed in a command and zoomed in the cameras, then zoomed in again. I felt the blood in my veins turn to ice as I identified it. It was a spherical object, some sort of gas giant by the looks of it. But what amazed me most was that, despite being surrounded by light, the planetoid itself was shrouded in darkness. No movement lay on its surface. It was as if it was frozen in time.

I imagined then what would happen when the blackness of our universe eventually made contact. I pictured the object erupting into a ball of flame as the concentrated gasses heated up and created a new sun. I realised then that additional planets must not be far ahead.

*Something for this sun to light,* I thought.

My mind lingered on this notion until Tyson's words moved about my mind as my eyes studied the stillness of the sphere.

*The face of God.*

I swallowed hard and took a shallow breath, adjusting my

gaze about the viewscreen. To the left of this unborn sun, far off in the distance, something appeared. I had hardly noticed it at first, but as it became larger with each passing second, it was impossible not to focus on.

I un-zoomed the camera as my heart thumped in my throat. The object continued to grow in size, despite the ship staying locked in the same position. Then, with a single blink, the object appeared before our craft.

To describe the object as a black ball of simultaneous beauty and horror would be a disservice to its brilliance. The only thing I could think of that would even remotely come close to classifying it was an iris.

As I struggled to categorise this object before me, I observed the inside of it begin to shift. Thousands of universes, moving as one. Their clouded arms fanned out, rotating until the eye had colours that I could not put into words.

The pupil dilated.

I could sense then the feelings of the entity. Disappointment and sorrow, but not surprise. No, this being was not surprised in the slightest, and I became aware that it had always known it would be found. Yet it hoped this event would not come to pass. A secret plea it had made with itself long ago.

A voice—or more accurately, an infinite number of voices—sprung forth inside my head. All in tandem, saying, "You see only a fraction of me now."

I knew each voice intimately, despite never hearing them before. They were everyone in my family tree, everyone from all the family trees of those who had existed, or would exist. But the ones that caused my brain to splinter were the voices of my children and their children's children. This gave me the hope that I would live on and somehow survive this moment. I wished to hear their voices in person and be far away from here when I did so.

"I made a promise to one of your species before," the entity started. "To tell you that the intricacies of life would be of little value, for you are not capable of understanding them. This has troubled your kind since I uttered it. But to you, I make this covenant. I will show you my face, and with it you will see the meaning of it all. I will use you to seed the beginning of the new attempt. Perhaps then, with such a thing imbedded so deeply, it will bring peace to those who follow."

"No—" I started to speak, but felt the voice roll over me once again.

"By coming here, you have agreed to this covenant. You had your warnings and yet you never heeded them."

I took my gaze from the eye of all creation and looked to Tyson, who still sat unconscious but upright, held in place by his flight harness. I struggled to understand what the entity meant. Tyson was no angel; he was a mortal like the rest of us.

The thought quickly abandoned me then, as I noticed how crude my surroundings looked. The bulkheads of the ship, the computer terminals, wiring running along the ceiling—dirty, jagged, unrefined. It all looked so primitive compared to the iris before me. Only Tyson and the hand that I slowly raised into view looked real, like something resembling creativity.

I lowered my hand and returned my attention to the entity. I could see the universes inside the pupil were rotating again. The iris began to grow larger as a second black dot raced towards me. The second dot arrived before I had time to process it was approaching me, and it too began to take the same shape. Millions upon millions of universes stirring inside it.

I could feel the blood flowing through my veins with each beat of my heart. Time was becoming meaningless as another black dot arrived, followed by another and another, and more and more. Each twisting into the shape of a pure, unbridled, blissful, torturous, immaculate, traumatising, perfect being.

My feeble human brain could not process such a sight and my cognitive function began to unravel. I could feel the electrons inside me separating, moving towards it. Cells disintegrating as atoms poured through the breaches of their walls. Consciousness flowing forward and back.

As my mind turned to dust and the electricity that had once served me joined the unfathomable entity, I saw the meaning of it all. All faculties of life, divided neatly before me. Life and death, limbo and beyond.

But the being had been right, I could not understand.

It was like trying to explain nuclear reactors to a garden snake, or parallel universes to a starfish. Except in this case, I was an ant, gazing into the next phase of universal evolution.

# A NOTE FROM THE AUTHOR

## Of Double Albums and Dreams Immaculate

As someone who has just completed this collection, you are no doubt wondering what I'm going on about in the subtitle of this note. To that I have to say, *A Stone's Throw Away From Paradise* was not the original title, nor did it share even the slightest resemblance to the anthology that you've just read. The original thesis for the book was two-fold: for it to be a "double-album," and for it to contain stories unlike what I had written before.

The notion of creating a double anthology stemmed from an obsession I experienced (and still do, to a certain extent) with the concept of the double album in music. The idea of having so much material that it cannot be contained on one disc of vinyl is something that fascinates me in a way I don't fully understand.

With this newfound space, one has the freedom to experiment, and more often than not, it is these experiments that allow the record to not only breathe, but be remembered. The Beatles' White Album is what really ensnared my mind with the concepts mentioned above. An album so versatile—so unique—that even fifty years later, many fans continue to have a hard time trimming it down to a single LP, which makes every person's attempt to do so unique.

In my blind ambition, I set out to make something impossible: the perfect double album. I wanted to break the mold of what most fans agreed on—that almost every double album could be trimmed down into a single album. I wanted to be the exception. Twenty-four stories, six on each "side," with each tale more fascinating than the last.

This idea fit perfectly with the stories I wanted to tell. I knew I wanted a collection that was different; stories of youthful nostalgia, the meaning of the soul, and the long walk that is the human condition. Stories that were more grounded, more everyday, more slices of life told by a yet-to-be-met friend.

Sure, some of the tales would have science-fiction elements, and some might even have shades of horror lurking within, but all would be very clearly unique to this project, which was then called *Dreams Immaculate*.

So, I did what any author worth their preverbal salt did. I wrote. I wrote a lot. I had the most productive year to date in writing. These writing sessions spawned stories that I knew would not work in *Dreams Immaculate,* but I tucked them aside for future collections.

Now, while I produced many more than twenty-four stories, I don't want to give you a false impression. It is not like I have some vault of finished novella-length tales sitting around in my notebooks. Several of the previously mentioned twenty-four stories were nothing more than flash fiction.

To give you another example of how ambitious this project was going to be, I originally planned to have a quote at the start of each story that would give a broader context to the themes found within. This idea barely got off the ground and I don't think I got more than a dozen or so quotes in total, many of which were junk. But there are three or four great ones that I have no doubt will appear in some form or another in the future.

As my debut novel, *A Monarch Among Kings,* entered the

editing phase, I continued to write more stories and become critical of the work I had penned for *Dreams Immaculate*. To my horror, I realised that I had fallen victim to the alluring siren call of the double album. Many of the stories in the collection were flab, self-indulgent dredge that could easily be jettisoned to make it a single collection.

It was then that the idea came to me. I could abandon the original outline of the project and trim the collection down to a single album and make it the best I had ever written. Cut the fat, clear the weeds, and leave only the jewel behind.

I took the three best quotes I had and used them to divide the collection into sections (Mind, Heart, and Soul, respectively). The stories were then divided up into their corresponding section based on their tone and themes.

This crash course in reconstructive surgery left me with fifteen stories. This was *Dreams Immaculate* for months before the unthinkable (but all too familiar) happened. I realised I was not happy with some of the stories that had survived the first round of cuts. I decided to tweak the project even more, removing some stories and extending the endings on a few of the tales that remained.

It was around this point I became all too aware that many of the stories I had created no longer fit the original idea of what *Dreams Immaculate* represented. I had done too much cutting. Had changed too much. The original thesis of the book was nothing like it had been when I had my epiphany several years back. I sat there, haunted, fearing that perhaps the whole project was a failure.

This wallowing did not last long, as I had another thought. By taking the best of *Dreams Immaculate* and combining them with the more science fiction-focused stories I was saving for a future anthology, I could make one hell of a collection. While I was at it, I figured I would take the title of that future collection and use it instead.

I began to move titles around in a Word document and

assemble a collection. It was not as many as I hoped, but it was enough to give me a newfound spark. I then began to write again, which coincidently lined up with the time period that *A Monarch Among Kings* was in the hands of my beta readers. It was in this phase that I introduced some new blood into the collection.

If you've gotten this far, then you can tell *A Stone's Throw Away From Paradise* has had a colourful and bloody history. I hope the stories that survived this grueling process shine all the brighter for it.

So, without further longwindedness, let's take a tour of the far side of these adventures and examine the structural bones, the underlying nature, and the messy set dressing that ties everything together.

**The Digital Zealot:**

This is a story that was written for the original version of *A Stone's Throw Away From Paradise*, before the amalgamation occurred and the project drastically changed shape. The idea of an ancient monastery built at the heart of a forest while a world-controlling A.I. is cognitively shackled in the basement, was a contrast that caught my attention one day and was too interesting a concept to focus on anything else.

It took me a few days to come up with the reasons for why the Old Machine would be sought out in the first place and why The Connection had ceased functioning, but once I had those concepts down, I wrote the story in a flash.

I'll be honest when I say this was the tale that I had the hardest time coming up with these "behind the scenes" notes for. There is a lot I wish to talk about, but to do so would be robbing you of the chance to interpret the story in your own way. I will say that the idea of machines inheriting religion and keeping the fire going, when their original creators abandoned such a covenant, is something that really stuck with me long after the story was penned.

## A Mother, a Child, and a Mystic:

This story continued to grow the most even after the first draft was written. Originally, the journey ended with the train derailment and the mother staring off into the tunnel.

That was the state the draft sat in for several months, until I realised that there was much more story to tell. I knew Wendy McDonald would not simply go home after something so life changing; she is far too determined of a person to do that. I knew she would seek out the mystic and question him on how he could have known such an event would happen.

Hemingway made a career of leaving his stories hanging just before a proper conclusion to let the reader fill in the gaps, and while I initially tried that approach with this story, I realised this was not the tale to attempt such a method on.

A year or so later, I wrote a different conclusion. This second attempt found the story ending as Wendy leaves the tent after saying her goodbyes. However, as I set the pen down, I realised that I was sitting on something much bigger than I had originally thought. An idea that could take the story from one that was middle of the pack, to something truly unique.

I had another scrap of a tale laying around called "My Favourite Memory," and I took some of the ideas from it and rounded off the conclusion for this story.

The notion of having a time machine and using it not to witness a historical event, but to visit a relative long gone really speaks to me. The creation of a new timeline where at least one of Brett's other versions can grow up with his mother beside him is something I'm sure many out there would choose, if given the chance.

**Soul Kitchens:**

One of the older stories in the collection, harkening from the original *Dreams Immaculate* sessions. The idea of angels lounging around listening to Twenties big band music really appealed to me.

In the original draft, there wasn't much to the tale besides the characters talking before work pulled them away, one by one.

The first few drafts left it vague as to why Edgar was not receiving any new contracts. It occurred to me in editing that I could add more detail to this idea by asking the question as to what happens to those guardian angels who unfortunately are paired with less-than-desirable souls? Not only that, but what such a pairing would do to not only to their psyche, but also their relationships with their coworkers?

I'm happy with the change of direction and feel it makes the story stand all the much taller for it.

**Of Winter Winds and Midlife Crises:**

The oldest story in the collection by a fair margin, written just before my move to British Columbia.

As I was penning the initial draft, I really had no idea where I was going and was just following the character through the snows with his daughter. As the story began to grow, the path became clear and I became aware of Harold's midlife crisis, his project at work, and that his siblings were coming over for the holidays.

The story originally ended with Harold telling his wife that he was going to spin the idea of the new laser to his brother. This would have been another Hemingway-inspired ending, letting the audience deduce what followed.

It didn't take long before I pictured a scene where Harold and Fred are working together out on the perimeter. I really wanted to not only show the scene, but also reveal to the audience that

Harold did get out of his rut and was happier than where he was at the start of the story.

When I was assigning this tale a spot in *Dreams Immaculate* and later *A Stone's Throw Away From Paradise*, I really liked how it brought the familiarity of a common problem to the forefront. While the other stories in the collection are dealing with cutting edge technology or god-like beings, here's a science fiction story that is dealing with one of the most fundamental issues of human existence. Even when humanity has achieved such a feat as the colonization of Mars, something as simple as the dreaded midlife crisis will still be the bane of many a citizen.

As a fun fact, the story had two working titles while I was crafting it: first, "Winter Winds" and then "A Crisis at Midlife." I decided to combine these titles into its current name and am pleased with the result.

**You Did This:**

This story was "written in the studio" (to borrow a term from the music industry). I knew I needed a twelfth tale after I had recently removed one from the collection for being too short.

It is worth noting that while "You Did This" was the last to be written, that didn't necessarily guarantee that it was to be included in the collection. There was a time when I thought about cutting it as well, as it is very dower in nature.

While it is indeed very downtrodden, I feel the ending is quite hopeful and optimistic. It often takes conflict for us as humans to realise the error of our ways, and this realisation can result in a positive outcome.

The problem here is that this is a work of fiction, and I don't believe that if the "button" was to ever be pushed, the universe would step in to save us. It is all the more likely that we will succumb to our nature and that the universe will have considered us an interesting experiment at best.

**An Epilogue to the Unfinished:**

This is a story that started off as an exercise to beat writer's block. I had been having a rough couple of days where nothing was coming to me, and I felt my muse had made a run for the hills. I wrote a story regarding this very idea and by the conclusion of it an idea had popped into my head where two people were going through a dead writer's manuscripts.

These couple of pages were all there was to the story for over a year, but as the idea stuck with me, I began to add more and more details to it. I was aware the writer was still lurking around, and I knew there were stories she was not fond of. This provided the real crux of the story. I wanted to explore where the line was between honouring the artist and straight up theft.

The question must be asked, would the creator have wanted the work to be released in its current state? After all, it was shelved for a reason. But on the other hand, there are the fans that deeply love the posthumously released works of their favourite artists, so does that mean their say is invalid?

The ending of the story is an idea I borrowed from a piece of flash fiction I had written, entitled "The Last Autograph." It was about a child who receives an autograph from an author, just minutes before the writer experiences an untimely death. Very depressing, I know, but the notion of possessing the last autograph a celebrity ever creates is something I thought was worth exploring. As I was coming up with the closing paragraphs to "An Epilogue to the Unfinished," I thought that using this idea from a relic of the *Dream's Immaculate* days would be a great way to close out the story.

**Upon a Pyramid:**

This too was a tale that started its life as nothing more than a few paragraphs. The first draft saw the protagonist sitting above the city, critiquing the holiday prepared by the species that worshipped it. It ended with an alien faction landing and the humans bowing to the newcomers instead.

While all of these concepts are included in the tale you're familiar with, to say I expanded on each of them is an understatement.

I flip-flopped on whether I should have Harmii actually appear in the narrative or strictly keep her as someone who is only mentioned. I ended up deciding that it would make the character's motivations that much more grounded if the audience met Harmii in person before she sets off on her doomed expedition. The scene in the bedchamber was created out of necessity to deliver on that idea. The scene essentially wrote itself, and Harmii was such an easy character to work with for it.

**The Train Station:**

This story holds the distinction of being the first I wrote upon moving to British Columbia.

Upon thinking up the idea, I originally struggled to figure out a way to have it make sense in the context of a real, functioning world. Questions like, "Why would everyone ride the train?" or "How could a train be sentient?" were things that held my pen back from meeting the page. However, I quickly realised that trying to explain how a fictitious world functions would kill the very magic of it. Sometimes stories just exist in their own fantastical lands. I decided to hone in on that and just tell the story as I saw fit.

**The Bonfire:**

I am a firm believer that the best horror comes from the places you least expect. It is this unexpectedness that makes the terror all the more impactful.

I'm not talking about jump scares—those are almost always telegraphed, and while the initial punch is alarming, it isn't exactly scary. No, true horror is something else entirely. It is in the pacing, the atmosphere, the mystery of the unknown. And of course it helps when we struggle to comprehend the entities that are encountered throughout.

I'm not proclaiming this story to be utterly terrifying, but I do feel that even from the onset, you, as the reader, can detect that something isn't right in this little farming community. I would dare venture to say that you cast aside the notion as you'd been lulled into a false sense of security by the stories prior, making the ending all the more unnerving.

Speaking of the ending, the original draft had no mention of the man with the "chilling, empty eyes," or a body being thrown in the fire. This change was incorporated in the edit as I thought it added another layer to the story and contributed to the overall creep factor I was going for in this one.

**A Changing of the Guard:**

I feel like most science fiction involving technology is bound to have an uprising of some sort. This event is usually violent and sudden in nature. While this is interesting from a narrative point of view, I don't necessarily believe it is entirely realistic.

I believe that the notion of "the great replacement" will come slowly, and while certain people will always oppose something, the vast majority of the population will accept the technology with open arms.

The idea of being the last human to work a job that has existed for hundreds, if not thousands of years is something that will undoubtedly become commonplace in the future. It will be one of those things that will be taught in history classes to children that will simply shrug, as they struggle to envision a world where artificial persons did not represent the bulk of the workforce.

**"Remember Us in Your Songs":**

An unspoken trope in fantasy is that orcs are evil. Everyone knows that one. They are ugly, vile, remorseless creatures who are about as cunning as a blunt axe.

For years now, I've wanted to tell a story where the orcs are not only the good guys, but brave and full of gallantry. A truly honourable race steeped in a rich history. A faction that we as humans should look up to, as we attempt to better ourselves. I know that in terms of traditional fantasy this idea must seem ludicrous to those purists out there, but I would be lying if I didn't say this was the starting point for the story.

As an aside, this concept was one that had followed me for many years. The struggle was to come up with a situation that would pit all these forces against each other in a convincing narrative structure and keep the pace of the battle entertaining. I am happy to finally see the story come to fruition.

**And to Dust You Shall Return:**

At the time of writing this one, I had eleven stories that I thought would be perfect for the anthology, but I was missing that twelfth story to round the collection off. I knew the story had to be a grand one. Something that tied the entire collection together.

I had the question of "What's at the end of space?" spinning around my mind for a while and decided to take that smidgen of a concept and roll with it.

As I set the pen down, I was extremely pleased with how it turned out and knew that it would be perfect to serve as the epic conclusion to the collection. How could any story follow up after the end and subsequent rebirth of all time, space, and the universe itself?

The tale had several titles that lunged out at me upon completion, "The Face of God" being the most obvious one. But several minutes later, I came up with the final title and knew that was the one.

———

And with that, we end our tour of the behind the scenes look at the stories from *A Stone's Throw Away From Paradise*. I hope there is at least one tale in this collection that sticks with you long after you put this book down. That is always my goal. Even better is if you found a story that has become your new favourite of mine. That is the motivation that keeps me going and serves as my muse.

Thank you for taking the tour with me; I'll let you off at the next stop. And who knows, maybe if enough people show interest in what *Dreams Immaculate* had originally looked like, it will prompt me to release the other stories from those sessions.

Until next time,

—Robert J. Bradshaw
April 2023

# WHAT'S NEXT FOR BRADSHAW?

Did you enjoy the anthology and can't wait to find out what I'm working on next?

In that case, I have some great news for you! My newsletter, "Bradshaw Monthly," has been going strong since December of 2020. On the $2^{nd}$ day of every month, I update my readers with such things as progress reports, the unveiling of cover art, and exclusive access to brand-new stories before they are available to the general public. But that, of course, is just scratching the surface.

Best of all? It's completely free! There has never been a better time than now to join the Bradshaw camp and subscribe. For easy access, head over to Facebook and search, "The Works of Robert J. Bradshaw" the link to my monthly newsletter is pinned to the top of my page. I hope to see you there!

Also as a side note, if you did enjoy the book, please consider leaving a review on Amazon, as it not only helps other people see the book in the algorithm but it also tells me what you enjoyed about my works.

# ACKNOWLEDGMENTS

If you read my author's note, you know this collection went through a great deal of changes and iterations before it assembled into the collection you just read through. As with all my previous works I wish to take the time to acknowledge all the people who stuck with me during this time and offered their support and encouragement every step of the way.

A very special thank you to my beta reader team of:

Colleen Atkinson, for her attention to details both great and small and grammar critiques on those all-too-familiar crutch words.

Dennis Atkinson, for always diving into my manuscripts the moment he receives them and providing some of the best character and narrative feedback a writer could ask for.

Veronica Martinez-Soto, for finding those small plot mistakes that I should have picked up on at some point during the numerous revisions, with food and drink consistency being her specialty.

I would also like to thank my creative team of:

My editor, Christie for all her great work and feedback. Her changes are always for the better and really give each passage that extra bit of bite with the structuring.

(As a side note, there is a reason editing has its own category at the Oscars—they really are the unsung heroes of many a great project. For reference, look at the rough cut of the original *Star Wars*. The editing made the movie into what we know today.)

My cover artist, Ronnie at *"Tegnemaskin.no"*, for taking my idea and truly running with it. He expanded on my notions in every way and really brought them to life.

I would like to take the time to also thank all those who have helped me along the way. Nathan Olmstead, Allison Tremblay, Adam Kudryk, Gabriela Hernandez Maltos, Alison Somerton, and Haley Sibernagel. I've said it before and I'll say it again: Just asking about my books and what I'm working on really helps in all aspects of the process, from vague idea to a published book. Thank you for all your support and continued interest in my latest projects.

To those above and the others who helped me unknowingly though the lengthy creative cycle of this project, I give you one last thank you from the bottom of my heart. Thank you for everything!

—Robert J. Bradshaw
July 2023

# ALSO BY ROBERT J. BRADSHAW

## SONGS OF THE ABYSS:

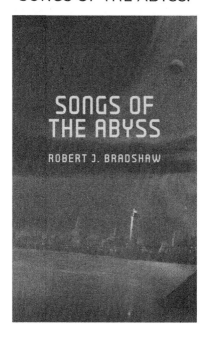

A creature that hates to be watched, a forest full of shapeshifting beings, and a war where the ordnance being dropped aren't bombs, but nightmares.

Ten stories of stunning science fiction, otherworldly horrors, and thrilling suspense. All coming together to form a collection like no other.

**Get your copy, today!**

## SHADOWS AT MIDNIGHT:

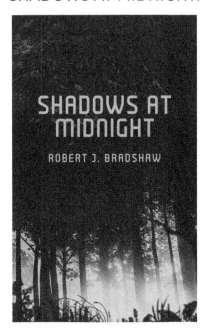

A Mayan ruin with a long-forgotten secret, a cult that is attempting to bridge the gap between worlds, and a beast that lurks inside the phone lines...

In this collection of tales, the mysteries only get darker.

Stories of horrors lurking in the depths, science fiction beyond imagination and pulse pounding thrills, coming together to create an anthology you won't be forgetting anytime soon.

**Get your copy, today!**

---

# A MONARCH AMONG KINGS

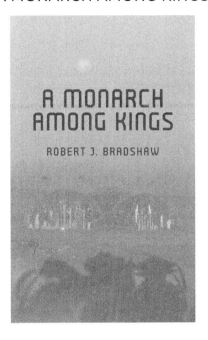

Far off in the Andromeda Galaxy, thousands of colonists have carved out a life for themselves on the remote world of Seryhenya.

However, as a young officer in the Colonial Guard Corps will soon discover, the planet might just hold more life than expected...

Follow multiple viewpoints as each character struggles to navigate the unfolding crisis. Some want to destroy this potential threat before it can fester; others want to live and let live. It is up for debate who is correct in their assessment of the situation.

But keeping an eye on the horizon might not be the only thing the colonists have to worry about...

**Get your copy, today!**

# ABOUT THE AUTHOR

Robert J. Bradshaw was born and raised in St. Catharines, Ontario, Canada. He relocated to British Columbia, seeking adventure. He currently lives in the Fraser Valley region.

*A Stone's Throw Away From Paradise* is Bradshaw's forth book penned to date. His other works include the anthologies *Songs of the Abyss* (released in 2020) and *Shadows At Midnight* (released in 2021). His debut novel, *A Monarch Among Kings*, a science fiction colonization epic, was released in 2022.

Bradshaw is currently hard at work on his sophomore novel, as well as another gathering of tales.

Printed in Great Britain
by Amazon